*He was beginning to wonder if he
hadn't made the biggest mistake
of his life . . .*

Casting his gaze around the hummock's rounded peak, Stillman found a handful of shell casings scattered in the grass. Scrutinizing one between his thumb and index finger, he saw it was a Springfield .45-70. Not the rarest of guns by any means, but the casing might come in handy in his identification of the gunman. He pocketed it and glanced back at the wagon, both horses dead on the trail.

He looked back toward the line of shacks and trees demarking town. "I'm going to get you, you son of a bitch!" he yelled, unable to contain his anger. Now he had an anonymous bushwhacker to add to his list of the day's grievous events, and to his growing catalog of problems that were his to solve on his way to taming a town.

As he made his way toward Clantick, rifle in hand, he was seriously beginning to wonder if coming here with Fay was the biggest mistake of his life.

ONCE MORE WITH A .44

Peter Brandvold

BERKLEY BOOKS, NEW YORK

This is a work of fiction. Names, characters, places, and incidents are either the product of the author's imagination or are used fictitiously, and any resemblance to actual persons, living or dead, business establishments, events or locales is entirely coincidental.

ONCE MORE WITH A .44

A Berkley Book / published by arrangement with the author

PRINTING HISTORY
Berkley edition / July 2000

The Penguin Putnam Inc. World Wide Web site address is http://www.penguinputnam.com

ISBN: 0-425-17556-1

BERKLEY®
Berkley Books are published by The Berkley Publishing Group, a division of Penguin Putnam Inc., 375 Hudson Street, New York, New York 10014.
BERKLEY and the "B" design are trademarks belonging to Penguin Putnam Inc.

PRINTED IN THE UNITED STATES OF AMERICA

10   9   8   7   6   5   4   3   2   1

"O, tell her, brief is life, but love is long."
—ALFRED LORD TENNYSON, *The Princess*

"There are demon-haunted worlds,
regions of utter darkness."
—THE UPANISHADS

1

Jody Harmon cantered his buckboard between the false fronts of Clantick, Montana Territory, and pulled up before the Pepin/Baldwin Mercantile. He turned to his wife, Crystal, who he had married two years ago but had known since they were both little taller than the grass growing on the slopes of the Two Bear Mountains.

Blond and blue eyed, with a splash of freckles across the bridge of her slender nose, Crystal wore her hair loose about her shoulders. She was the most beautiful girl Jody had ever seen—not that he'd seen that many, having grown up on Montana's Hi-Line, never traveling farther south than Great Falls or farther north than Medicine Hat, in the Canadian Territories.

Still, the former Crystal Johnson was a piece of work. Pretty as a speckled pup but tough and boyish in a feminine sort of way, she worked right alongside Jody on their ranch, as capable as any hand on the Hi-Line. The only thing she lacked was housecleaning skills—oh, Lordy, could she let the cabin go!—but she made up for it in spades in cooking, wrangling, tanning, and all other areas of their lives.

"What the hell are you looking at?" she asked Jody now, with twinkling eyes and a mocking, impudent smile.

"You," Jody said with a grin.

"I see that. Would you mind telling me why?"

His smile thinned but his eyes remained sharp. "I'm crazy about you."

Crystal poked the brim of her flat-brimmed hat up and inclined her head. "I think all that bouncin' on the road's made you randy. You just better get your mind out of your pants and on your chores, Mr. Harmon, before I have to call the sheriff."

"We could take a little break in that cottonwood grove down by the river," Jody said, his eyes turning playfully lascivious.

"I do need to call the sheriff!"

Jody slid closer to her on the seat, and put an arm around her shoulders. "Don't be hasty now, my little honeybunch. What I got in mind for you might just have you howlin' like a she-bitch for more."

In spite of herself, Crystal snickered and made a half-hearted attempt at wrestling out of his grasp. "Jody . . . people can hear you. . . ."

"We'll have us a little repeat of what we did over mornin' coffee."

Crystal squelched a squeal. "Oh, no, we won't!" She pulled back, trying to contain her giggling as Jody nuzzled her neck. She tossed her eyes around to see if anyone was watching and saw a stoop-shouldered man in a threadbare suitcoat and floppy-brimmed hat strolling hangdoggedly down the boardwalk. The walk was unmistakable.

Crystal's tone became serious. "Jody, stop. Daryl Bruner's headed this way."

Jody continued nibbling her right ear. "Who?"

"Daryl. Stop it now!" She pushed him away with both hands. Jody sighed and turned to see the big man come to a halt above them, on the mercantile's loading dock. He was carrying what appeared to be a small suitcase.

Daryl spread his girlishly wide, full lips with a simpleminded grin. Thirty-three but with the mind of a ten-year-old, Daryl Bruner was known as the town idiot. Story had it that when he was a kid he was hit in the head by chimney bricks when a tornado swept through town. His uncle was a blacksmith and part-time drummer, and every Saturday Daryl followed him around Clantick, pitching everything from elixirs to pots and pans.

"Hi, Jody. Hi, Crystal. What are you two doin'?"

Jody glanced at Crystal, grinning. Crystal met the glance with a half-grin of her own, and returned her gaze to Daryl. "We just came to town to load up supplies, Daryl. The larder's getting a little empty these days. What are you up to?"

"Uncle Ebben an' me, we're goin' door-to-door with some of the prettiest jewels I bet you ever seen. Wanna see?" Daryl's head was tucked low in his shoulders, and he regarded Crystal and Jody with utmost seriousness from below his bushy black eyebrows.

Crystal shifted position on the seat to glance at the suitcase. "Yeah, what do you have? My birthday's comin' up soon, and Jody needs to be shoppin' for a present."

Jody gave a grunt as Daryl lifted the suitcase in his big arms, tripped the latches, and carefully opened the lid with one hand while supporting the suitcase with his other arm. "See?" he said, voice filled with genuine awe.

Crystal lifted her head to look at the cut-glass costume jewelry and cameos mounted on cardboard covered with black velvet. "Ooo, some fine-lookin' stuff," Crystal cooed, hoping Daryl wouldn't detect any falseness in her tone. "How much?"

Daryl touched each bauble with a thick finger as he read off the prices scribbled on a small white card pasted to the inside of the suitcase's lid. "Fine-lookin' stuff at a steep price," Jody lamented. "Too bad I just have cash enough to fill my supply list today."

"Cheapskate!" Crystal said, wrinkling her brows at him playfully.

"I tell you what I do have, though, Daryl," Jody said, fishing in his pocket for a coin. "I do have a nickel you can lay down for a mug of beer . . . when you're through for the day, of course," he added seriously.

Daryl's love for beer was famous throughout the county, and no one begrudged him that refuge. An eminently gentle creature, he'd never been known to harm anyone or anything; in fact, he befriended every stray dog and cat that wandered up to his uncle's blacksmith shop. To a grubliner a few years ago, he'd given the very shirt off his back.

"Oh, gosh! Why—thank you, Jody!" he said, wasting no time in closing the suitcase, securing the latches, and accepting the coin from Jody's outstretched hand. "I . . . I thank you mighty kindly."

Bowing like a Chinaman, he tipped his hat to Crystal and continued down the boardwalk, the torn sole of his right shoe flapping as he walked.

"Don't go spending that nickel till you're done working for your uncle," Jody called after the manchild.

Daryl turned around and grinned and continued on his way.

Crystal said to Jody, "From the look on his face you'd swear he'd just made his biggest sale of the day."

"Unless you knew him," Jody allowed, watching Daryl step off the boardwalk and half run across the street, in front of a mule drawn dray stacked high with milled lumber. "Well, I reckon I best get to it . . . unless you changed your mind about a little side trip down to the river, that is."

Crystal rolled her eyes and climbed down from the wagon. "I'll head over to the gun shop and pick up the ammo we're needing."

"Meet me back here, then?"

Crystal nodded. " 'Bout ten minutes."

"Sounds good. You can help me load the flour." Jody smiled.

"No, I thought I'd have Mrs. Hall help me pick out a dress for the birthday bash I just know you're gonna line up for me."

Jody shook his head and headed for the door of the mercantile. "You sure do get some crazy ideas in your head, Crystal Harmon."

He went on into the store and Crystal waited for a surrey to pass. She waved to the feather-hatted woman driving it, then jogged across the street, holding her flat-brimmed hat on her head with one hand.

She mounted the boardwalk and turned the corner around the tonsorial parlor, heading down a side street, where several shops had gone up in recent months. Some were so new you could still smell the pine resin in the wood.

Two rough-looking cowboys milling before a saloon gave her lascivious stares. She tried to ignore them, but the boldness of the men's looks and the depraved way they curled their lips at her was rather shocking. She hadn't seen the men around before, so she assumed they were newcomers. The railroad and the great expanse of prime grazing land in the area was attracting all kinds to Clantick and the Hi-Line. Crystal knew it was progress, but she didn't like how rough the area was becoming in the process. There were bar fights and shootings nearly every night; and an angry mob had hanged an Indian down by the river just last month. Not only that, but a few months ago, the telegrapher found the county sheriff dead in one of his own jail cells—murdered.

This wasn't the town Crystal remembered from her childhood, and she resented the way the hair now pricked on the back of her neck as she made her way down the boardwalk to the gun shop, the two strange cowboys staring after her.

"That pretty little cowgirl can take me for a ride any day of the week," one of them muttered loudly enough for her to hear.

Crystal stiffened with anger and almost stopped and turned around but decided against it. Letting such men get to her was exactly what they wanted. They wanted her to turn around, so they could humiliate her further. She'd been through it before in recent weeks, with just such men as these. Nothing she could do or say could morally cow them; it would only encourage them.

She crossed the side street, climbed the boardwalk,

and turned into Hallum's Gun Sales and Repair, the bell jingling over the door as she did.

Julius Hallum poked his head through the curtain leading to the back room. He was a medium-sized gentleman with dark wavy hair parted on the side and a full brown mustache. The leather apron he wore was soiled with grease and gun oil.

"Well, good mornin' to you, Crystal! What brings Mrs. Jody Harmon to town this fine Saturday?"

"Hi, Mr. Hallum."

Hallum frowned as he pushed through the curtain and set his fists on the glass-topped display case. "Say, you don't look so good. Something wrong?"

Crystal wasn't looking at him. Her eyes were on the display case, but her brain was not registering the assortment of revolvers displayed there, on a bed of red velvet. "Oh, just some stupid hammerheads down the street. I just let 'em get to me is all."

Hallum scowled, pursing his lips and nodding his head. "Over at the Goliad?"

Crystal nodded.

"Yeah, that place has really been attracting trouble lately," the gunsmith loudly lamented. "All the rough-shods from miles around have settled in there, just across the street from me. It's bad for business. Gets so that decent folks don't like to walk this way to visit my store, so they do all their buyin' at one of the mercantiles."

"The town's growing," Crystal said, shrugging her shoulders and giving a sigh. "I guess it's bound to grow bad as well as good."

"Yeah, I guess it comes with the territory. If you ask me, though, I think we need another sheriff in town."

"Ralph Merchant isn't working out?"

"Hah!" Hallum cried. "I hardly ever see the man, and not too many other people do, either. I think he spends most of his time hunting in the mountains. Those elk, they don't mouth off or shoot back, you know."

"Right," Crystal said, wagging her head.

"Well, enough of my bellyaching. What can I do ya for?"

Crystal pointed at the boxes stacked on the shelves behind the counter. "Couple boxes of those thirty-thirties, and one of the forty-fours."

"Comin' right up," Hallum said, turning and waving a hand around as he searched for the right caliber. Finding them, he plucked them from their respective stacks and set them on the counter with his customary flourish. "Any twenty-twos?"

"No, thanks."

"Oil?"

"Not today."

"Well, I'm grateful you braved this end of town for me, Crystal. I hope you'll continue to do so . . . in spite of the bad element that's moved in. I need the business."

Crystal pursed her lips with a halfhearted smile. "Well, as long as you keep your guns and ammo cheaper than Mr. Hall, I'll keep doin' business with you, Mr. Hallum. Jody says I'd walk an extra mile in a blizzard so I could save a penny off a spool o' thread."

Hallum laughed. "Speaking of Jody, how's that little Remington working out for him?"

Before Crystal could answer, men's voices rose up the street. Someone yelled out, whooping and yelling in what sounded like the taunting fashion of a schoolboy.

Crystal turned and moved to the window, looking up the street in the direction from which she'd come. Several men had spilled out of the Goliad saloon and into the street, spooking the horses tethered to the hitch rack.

Julius Hallum walked out from behind the counter and joined Crystal at the window. "More trouble at the Goliad," he said fatefully.

"I reckon," Crystal said. Watching the men gather in the street behind the skittering horses, Crystal frowned and tipped her head for a better look. She moved to the door and opened it.

"You best stay in here until the storm passes, Crystal," Hallum advised.

Ignoring the man, Crystal stepped onto the boardwalk, letting the door rattle shut behind her. She stood there and appraised the situation on the street.

It appeared that two men, the very two men she'd passed earlier, one of whom had made the lewd comment, were trying to goad another man into a fight. Crystal couldn't see the other man clearly, because the two ruffians were in the way, backing the third man farther into the street.

One of the two ruffs was carrying what appeared to be a suitcase. Studying it, Crystal saw that it was the same suitcase Daryl Bruner had been packing.

2

Crystal's heart jerked and her stomach churned as she stepped out into the street for a better look.

Behind her she heard the door of the gun shop open and out of the corner of her eye saw Julius Hallum step cautiously onto the boardwalk. Crystal tilted her head to look around the shoulder of one of the two men goading the third, and saw what she'd feared.

The man the two ruffs were trying to push into a fight was Daryl Bruner.

Crystal's face flushed with anger and her knees shook.

Daryl was backing away from one of the men, wringing his big hands together and staring at the crowd of cowboys before him with fearful, haunted eyes.

"You wanna tell me one more time what you called me in there, retard!" yelled one of the ruffs, a small, wiry man in a plaid flannel shirt and hat with a funneled brim.

"I . . . I . . . didn't call you nothin'," Daryl said, so softly that Crystal could barely hear him.

"Yes, you did, you big stupid oaf! You called me a no-good cat-kicker—that's what you called me, you no-good, brainless wonder!" The small man grinned at the bigger man beside him.

"No, he didn't say that, Rafe," the bigger man said. "He called you a *lousy,* no-good cat-kicker." The bigger man turned to the smaller man, and Crystal could see his grinning profile.

One of the cowboys standing on the boardwalk piped up. "An' all 'cause ya kicked that mangy cat the bartender feeds!"

"All right, Bruner, your time is up," the firebrand at the head of the pack said. "You got a pistol?"

Grinding her teeth together, Crystal moved toward the crowd and yelled, "That's enough! Leave him alone!"

Only a couple of men from the crowd turned their eyes to her. One said, "Stay out of this, miss," and turned back to the show.

The firebrand taunting Daryl turned to the man next to him. "Billy, give the retard your gunbelt. No one's gonna say I shot an unarmed man."

Crystal was still moving toward the crowd, making a bee-line from the middle of the street. Glancing around, she saw several businessmen standing in the doorways. Half-consciously she expected their help, but none of them moved from their doorsteps. Crystal shuddered to think what would happen if Daryl strapped on the gunbelt the big man was carrying over to him.

"Daryl, don't do it!" she yelled as she reached the crowd's perimeter and started pushing through, trying to get to Daryl.

One of the men in the crowd stepped in her way. "You just butt out of this, little missy," he said sharply. "This ain't none of your affair. That big retard just got smart with Rafe, an' it's time he learned his lesson."

"It sounded to me like a pretty harmless insult," Crystal said.

"Yeah, that's how they start," the big man said. He'd

just delivered his gunbelt to Daryl and was returning to stand beside his friend, the smaller man called Rafe.

Daryl stood alone in the middle of the street, holding the gunbelt as though it had suddenly materialized from thin air, as though it were a snake writhing in his fist.

"You go ahead and wrap that belt around your waist and buckle it," Rafe instructed.

Crystal had never felt so angry. Her vision was beginning to swim and her knees felt weak. "Goddamnit!" she suddenly shrieked. "That's *enough*! Daryl, just walk away!"

She took a step toward the man in front of her and brought her right boot up savagely, kicking the man squarely in his unprotected crotch. The man let out a scream and doubled over, turning sideways and falling to his knees.

Crystal brushed past him. She'd taken two steps when the back of a big hand slammed into her face. She staggered backward, the sharp pain shooting through her nose and cheek, her eyes watering, and then she fell back.

She must have lost consciousness for at least thirty seconds because she was only dimly aware of feet moving away from her, then a heavy silence followed by the sound of a single man's voice. The voice was low and quiet but sinister. Then a pistol shot rang out, like a big balloon popping. Crystal pushed herself onto her elbows. Her head swirled, and she saw double.

"We best get the hell out of here," a man said.

"Hey, it was a fair fight. He went for the gun," another man said.

"Yeah, but just the same, Rafe, I think we best get back to the ranch."

Crystal heard the squeak of saddle leather as the men mounted their horses and spurred their mounts into the street, heading out of town. She saw them out of the corner of her eye, felt the ground vibrate with the pounding hooves. Her attention was on the body lying in the street.

"Oh, Daryl," she whispered, and pushed herself to her knees, then her feet, feeling her bruised lip swelling and a sharp pain in her cheekbone, where the man had struck her.

She made her way to the body and knelt down, a great sadness washing over her, threatening to pull her back down. There was a blood spot the size of her hand in the middle of Daryl's chest, and in the middle of the spot was a small, round hole which seemed to be sucking in the shirt. The shirt soaked up most of the blood; the rest ran inside his coat and onto the ground.

Tears welled out of Crystal's eyes, and she lowered her head, taking the dead man's hand in hers.

"Crystal!" someone yelled from up the street.

She lifted her head to see Jody through the veil of tears. He ran toward her with the rifle he'd stowed in the buckboard. He did not normally carry a sidearm, believing, like his father, the late Bill Harmon, that guns were more apt to attract trouble than deflect it.

"They killed Daryl!" Crystal cried, lips trembling and tears running down her face.

Jody was kneeling beside her now, his eyes darkening, his face blanching, as he gazed down at the body. "Who did—?" he started, his voice catching. "Who in the hell would do such a thing?"

"I don't know who it was. I've never seen the man before. A cowboy, though. They were all cowboys."

"All?"

"There were several."

"Jesus Christ," Jody hissed, standing and grating his teeth. He looked down the street where the dust from the fleeing horses was still settling.

Drawn by the single gunshot from the main section of town, several people had come down the side street to stand around Jody and Crystal and the prone body of Daryl Bruner.

"Someone go get the sheriff," Jody said to one of the men.

"No need—I'm here," came a gruff voice. Jody turned and saw Sheriff Ralph Merchant push through the circle of onlookers, trailed by Julius Hallum, who had apparently fetched him.

Merchant was a rough-looking man with stringy hair falling out of his worn slouch hat. He was broad-shouldered and slim-hipped, but he boasted a paunch that nearly turned his belt buckle upside down. Hailing from Kansas, he'd been a cowboy most of his life. When the rheumatism had kept him from sleeping on the cold ground, he landed the sheriff's job in the little berg of Big Sandy, twenty miles south. He'd accepted the job as Clantick's sheriff three years later, when the previous lawman, Chester Early, was found tied to a bunk in one of his own jail cells, with his throat cut. No one else had wanted the job.

The problem was Ralph Merchant was an easygoing

cowboy, not a sheriff. He did not have the steel needed to cool the boiling cauldron the once peaceful Clantick was now becoming.

Crystal told him the story of how Daryl had been killed, and Julius Hallum corroborated it. Ralph Merchant stepped away from the crowd, tipped back his sweat-stained hat with a sausage-sized finger, and gazed down the street, in the direction the cowboys had fled. He had a perplexed, unconfident look on his big, red face. His nose was swollen by years of hard drinking.

"Anybody know who they were or where they're from?" he asked the crowd in general.

No one said anything for several seconds. Then a woman in the crowd piped up. Crystal didn't recognize her but could tell by her dress that she was a pleasure girl from the Goliad.

"The one that shot Bruner there's name is Rafe. He rides for Norman Billingsley. So do most of the others he was with. Don't tell him I said nothin', though. He's an ornery son of a bitch, Rafe."

Crystal found herself staring at the woman. The woman gave her a heated look and said in a pinched, sarcastic voice, "Pardon my French." Then she lifted her skirts, stepped onto the boardwalk, and disappeared through the swinging doors of the Goliad.

"What are you going to do, Sheriff?" Jody asked Merchant.

The potbellied man didn't say anything for several seconds. Then he turned his neck sharply and inclined his head, as if to work out a charley horse, and said through a sigh, "Well, I guess I better go out and have me a talk with Mr. Billingsley."

He looked at Jody. "Harmon, can you get the under-taker for young Bruner here?"

"Sure thing," Jody said.

The sheriff turned and started back to the jail for his horse, and Jody watched him go. The man was as bull-legged as they came. Jody turned to Crystal, who was staring down at Daryl.

"They shot him right out here in the street . . . just 'cause he got after them for kicking a cat," she said.

"What happened to your face?"

"I tried to stop 'em," Crystal said thinly.

"Come on, honey," Jody said to her gently, taking her by the arm and leading her toward the boardwalk. "You sit down and wait for me here, while I go fetch Doc Evans and his hearse."

"That Rafe better hang for what he did to Daryl," Crystal said.

"The sheriff will get him," Jody told her, and started away.

Will he? Crystal wondered when Jody had left. She was sitting there alone on the boardwalk, staring at the body. The crowd had started to disperse. A few men who knew Daryl's uncle stood shaking their heads nearby. The saddle maker, Ivan Sanderson, threw a rock at a dog that sniffed too close to Daryl's body.

Crystal asked herself if Ralph Merchant could get the job done . . . or would Clantick just keep getting more and more wild, more and more savage and mean?

She didn't like the answer she came up with.

Something had to be done.

3

Ben Stillman sat in the jostling day coach as the train sped northeastward into the mid-afternoon of a warm June day.

His wife, the former Fay Beaumont, napped against the window, one long leg crossed over the other, her lovely black hair curling down from the pillow the conductor had provided. There were no sleeping cars available on the line up from Butte, where they'd switched trains, so they'd had to make do with the stiff seats of the train's single day coach.

Stillman didn't mind. He'd spent half his life sleeping on the ground. He knew Fay didn't, either—she may have been born to a wealthy French rancher, but she could rough it as well as any drover; she saw it as an adventure, in fact—but Stillman always felt the doting urge to make his beautiful wife of two years as comfortable as he possibly could.

That's why a frown furrowed his brow now as he stared fondly at the pretty woman in a deep burgundy traveling dress with matching wool vest, a feathered hat of the same color, and a beaded reticule resting in her lap. How would she fare on the Hi-Line? So much bad had happened to her there, before she and Stillman were married. Would unhappy memories of that past life with the depraved Donovan Hobbs, her former husband, haunt her? Also, Clantick, the little town on the Hi-Line to which they were returning after a two-year absence, was so remote and, as Jody Harmon had said in his letter imploring Stillman to come, wild.

Fay had always been a good sport. She saw life as an adventure, no matter where it took her. But she was a curious, precocious young woman who needed libraries, book stores, museums, and educated conversation over afternoon tea or late-night brandy.

Could she flourish in the wild, hell-for-leather town that Clantick had apparently become? Could she grow, mentally and spiritually, in such a remote place as Montana's northern Hi-Line country? Could she—here was the question that really haunted him—find true satisfaction married to a career lawman like Ben Stillman?

Stillman pondered the question and stared at his lovely wife, who slept with a slight smile on her wide, full lips. Her eyelids moved a little as she dreamed.

Finally, antagonized by all his uncertainties about bringing Fay back to the Hi-Line, Stillman could no longer sit still. He stood slowly, careful not to wake her, and moved clumsily down the aisle, between the rows of gambling cowboys, dozing drummers, and immigrant farm families, grabbing the seat backs for balance.

When he made the door, he stepped through it onto the vestibule, where the wind nearly caught his ten-gallon hat. He grabbed it and snugged it down tighter on his head, noticing that the conductor, Ted March, was leaning on the rail having a smoke. March turned to him fumbling with the brass buttons of his blue wool uniform, which he must have undone to give his prominent belly a breather while he smoked.

"At ease, Ted, at ease," Stillman cooed, standing under the car's overhang to roll a cigarette.

"Oh . . . hi, Ben," the conductor said, relaxing with a sigh. "Thought maybe you were one o' those businessmen from back East. A man doesn't wanna be out of uniform when one of them comes out to complain about the rough ride or how behind schedule we are. Might complain to my superiors about my unkempt person and such." March shook his head.

"Ain't it time you're gettin' out o' this racket?" Stillman asked him. "Hell, Ted, I knew you back when we were all huntin' buffalo, and you were no spring chicken then."

"I got too many goddamn mouths to feed."

"You mean your kids haven't grown up and left home?" Stillman asked. He licked the edge of the paper and rolled the cigarette closed.

The conductor took a drag off his own quirley. "Yeah, I got all my own growed up, but now my sister and her brats have moved in with me and Edna in Helena. Her husband was a brakeman. He got drunk and fell off a vestibule. Reached out to grab the rail and the train sucked him under. Cut him in four pieces. When they dragged him out and boxed him up, he looked like a roast all sliced for Sunday dinner."

March ran a thick, red hand down his gray-bearded face that reminded Stillman a little of pictures of Rip Van Winkle. "So, anyway, we have Arlene and her three with us now, and the oldest ain't but eleven."

"Damn the luck," Stillman said.

"Damn the luck is right." March looked at Stillman and squinted his eyes curiously. "What brings you back this way? I heard you were working for Pinkerton out in Denver."

"I was, but a month ago I got a letter from Jody Harmon up to Clantick. You probably don't know Jody, but he's Bill Harmon's boy."

"Milk River Bill? You don't say! Bill was killed, wasn't he—?" March stopped himself. He remembered that Bill Harmon had been killed during that fuss up on the Hi-Line two years ago, the cattle and land war instigated by Fay Stillman's former husband, Donovan Hobbs.

It was a sad story, and March wasn't sure Stillman wanted to be reminded of it.

"Yeah, Bill was killed two years ago," Stillman groused, looking off at the rolling landscape, which appeared washed out under the harsh afternoon light—pastures dotted with cattle, spring fields showing green with sprouting wheat and oats, and here and there a gray cabin hunkered under cottonwoods near a creek and a windmill. Red-winged blackbirds quarreled in the cattails along sloughs still swollen with snowmelt.

"Anyway," Stillman continued, "Jody wrote me a letter about a month ago. He wanted me to come up to Clantick and take the sheriff's job."

"Yeah, I heard they lost another one—sheriff, I mean," March said. "That town's become as wild as Dodge City back when Texas cowboys were still coming in with their longhorns!"

"That's what Jody said."

"He wants you to clean up the town?"

Stillman shrugged self-effacingly. "I guess so. I thought about it for a while, then I wrote back and told him I'd give it a try. I just couldn't say no to the boy. He and Crystal—that's his wife—are like family to me. The kids I never had."

"So you quit Pinkerton's?" March raised his eyebrow at this. Pinkerton's was a highly respected detective agency, and anyone working for them—mostly ex-lawmen like Stillman—had a plush, well-paying job.

"That wasn't so hard," Stillman said. He looked off again. "I just didn't fit in there. They had me workin' a desk job on account of the bullet in my back, and I just never really got used to city life."

The thought made him feel guilty, because he knew that Fay had taken well to Denver. She'd met quite a few people with her refined tastes and civilized interests. And while she'd supported him in his decision to return to Clantick—she'd even encouraged him, knowing how he'd disliked the Pinkerton job—he felt like a heel for tearing her away from civilization so he could go back to the wild and wooly frontier.

"So it's once more with a forty-four, eh, Ben?" March said, glancing at the Army Colt holstered butt-forward on Stillman's left hip.

"I reckon so," Stillman warily allowed, wondering if he still had it in him. He was forty-six years old, and the bullet he'd taken in the back from a drunk whore in Virginia City, when he'd been a deputy U.S. marshal of Montana Territory, was still lodged right where she'd put it, hugging his spine. The surgeons hadn't dared go near it and risk putting Stillman in a wheelchair.

March flicked his cigarette over the rail of the vestibule and offered Stillman his hand. "Well, good luck to you, Ben."

Before Stillman could shake his hand, an enormous explosion sounded from somewhere ahead of the train. Stillman jerked a look over the roof of the car opposite and saw thick black smoke billowing in the distance.

Then, suddenly, the train's brakes were applied with a high-pitched, teeth-grinding shriek, and Stillman and March were thrown forward into the rear of the express car. March lost his hat and the wind grabbed it as he cursed, clutching his shoulder, which had taken the brunt of the impact.

Stillman found himself on his butt, with his back against the door of the car he'd been riding in. He could hear screaming and yelling from inside the train. As the train was still grinding to a slow, hard-fought halt, he heard what could only have been the popping of guns coming from the area of the explosion.

He knew instantly that the train was under attack by robbers. He looked at March as the train shuddered to a stop, and he recovered his balance.

"You all right, Ted?"

March was pulling himself to his feet. "What in Sam Hill . . . !"

"I think we're being robbed," Stillman yelled back, above the popping of guns and the yelling of passengers, who were opening windows and sticking their heads out for a look. "Are you armed?"

"Hell, no, I'm not armed!" March responded angrily. "We ain't had a robbery in months, and guns only make the passengers jittery."

"Then you better lay low," Stillman said. "I'll be right back."

He had to make sure Fay was all right before he could

do anything about the robbery. To that end, he went back into the car and moved briskly down the aisle, telling everyone to remain seated and calm and to get their heads back inside unless they wanted them blown off.

Stillman was relieved to see Fay, standing before her seat amid the agitated crowd. Her hair was disheveled and her face was pale with fear, brown eyes dark with worry, but they brightened when she saw him.

"Ben, what happened?" she said as he approached.

"We're being held up," Stillman said, taking her into his arms, relieved to find her well. "They must have blown the tracks ahead of the train. Are you all right?"

"I'm fine," she said. "What are we going to do?"

"I'm gonna head back up and see if I can do anything. They're probably in the express car. You stay here and try to get everyone to calm down, will you?"

Fay's eyes filled with worry. "Ben, you can't go up there!"

"I'm just going to see if there's anything I can do. I won't try anything stupid—I know I'm outgunned." Stillman kissed her lips, staring into her eyes. "I'll be back."

"Ben, please . . ."

He'd just started back down the aisle when the door to the vestibule opened and two rough-looking hombres entered wearing burlap hoods with the eyes and mouths cut out. One man wielded a sawed-off, double-barreled shotgun. The other held a revolver. A woman screamed, but the rest of the passengers in the car fell silent.

Stillman cast a look at the rear of the car and saw another man, dressed like the first two, enter with another shotgun. He stood there like a sentinel, the butt of the shotgun on his hip.

"All right, everybody just sit down and keep your mouths shut," shouted the man with the pistol. "Anybody gets any funny ideas about being a hero, forget about it unless you wanna go out in a hail of lead! Just hand over all your money and jewelry when my buddy comes by with his sack, and we'll be on our way. Anybody holdin' out on us gets a bullet in the eye. Understood?"

The man with the shotgun moved down the aisle, shotgun in one hand, the open bag in the other. "All right, stop thinkin' about it now, and cough it up. Every bit of it! Hurry up, let's go. We ain't got all day!"

Men fumbled for their wallets and women opened their purses and dumped them into the bag as the man approached their seats yelling, keeping the fear up, threatening to kill anyone who decided to hold onto Grandma's wedding ring or their prized pocket watch. If he so much as thought anyone was holding back something valuable, he'd shoot first and ask questions later.

Meanwhile, a baby cried and an old woman somewhere behind Stillman whimpered into her handkerchief.

Stillman sat in his seat beside Fay, about three-quarters of the way down the aisle, and considered his options. He could attempt a shot at the man with the bag. If he hit him and killed him, he could then shoot the man at the front of the car, who stood, pistol in hand, watching the passengers, making sure no one tried to play hero.

The only problem with Stillman's plan was that if he didn't kill each man with his first two shots, passengers were liable to get killed. If he sat tight and let the robbers go about their business, chances were no one would die.

It was true that some people here were probably losing their life savings—some were no doubt farmers heading west to start a new life, every cent they owned nestled deep in the pockets of their homespun pants—but it was better than losing their lives. Besides, a posse could be rounded up later, and there was always the possibility the bandits would be caught and the loot recovered.

But it wasn't going to go as smoothly as Stillman had hoped. The man with the shotgun had stopped before a feeble old man who was apparently unwilling to part with his watch.

"Come on, hand it over, Gramps!" the man with the shotgun shouted.

"No . . . I . . . can't," the old man returned.

"Grampa, *please*," begged the little girl sitting beside him.

"If you don't hand it over, Pops, I'm gonna shoot this girl in her pretty little head!"

This had gone far enough.

Stillman stood casually, almost as though he were about to stretch.

"Hey," the masked man behind him said, sounding more irritated than spooked.

That's what Stillman had wanted. Before the man leveled the shotgun, Stillman deliberately drew his Colt Army, extended his arm toward the rear of the car, aimed quickly but carefully, and shot the man through the forehead. The two men toward the head of the car were slow to react, their attention having been on the old man with the watch.

Stillman turned the Colt on the man with the bag and fired just as the man dropped the loot and was lowering the shotgun's barrel to his left hand for support. Stillman's Colt barked and spit flames. The man flew backward into a drummer's lap, a hole through his blue flannel shirt spouting blood.

Both men were dead in less than a second after Stillman had stood.

The third man, with the pistol, came running down the aisle. "Why you lousy goddamn—!" Stillman cut his sentence off with a .44 slug through the shoulder of the man's shooting arm.

The man fired his pistol, but the bullet chunked through the floor. The man dropped to a knee, screaming and cursing and ripping off his mask. He looked to his right and grabbed the girl sitting there, jerking her in front of him before Stillman could squeeze off another shot. The man held the girl with his wounded right arm. With his left hand, he brought a wide-bladed butcher knife to her throat.

"Drop it, asshole!" the man shrieked, spittle flecking off his lips, eyes wide and crazy, hair a tangled mess around his head. "I'm gonna carve up this girl like a Thanksgivin' turkey!"

"You don't wanna do that," Stillman said, moving slowly up the aisle toward them.

The girl's mother was screaming, and the father was holding her back as she fought to lunge for her daughter. The car was buzzing with fervent groans and gasps.

"You drop that gun right now, or I swear I'll cut her!" the outlaw intoned.

Calming himself with steady, even breaths, Stillman swallowed and shook his head. "I can't let you do that, friend. Now, let the girl go."

"I'm gonna *cut* her!" the man yelled through a hideous laugh.

Just before the blade's pointed tip broke through the tender skin of the girl's neck, Stillman sighted down the Colt's barrel and fired. The man fell like a carcass cut from a rope. The girl lunged for her parents, screaming.

Stillman moved forward, grabbed the knife out of the outlaw's hand, and saw that his bullet had gone cleanly through the man's right eye, killing him instantly.

Stillman was about to run up the aisle when he saw Ted March enter looking pale but pleased. "Now, that was some shootin'!" the conductor said, and whistled.

"Are there any more bandits?" Stillman asked urgently.

March shook his head. "There were two more on horses, but they hightailed it when they heard the shootin'. I don't think they had much stomach for a fight." He chuckled.

Stillman turned. Several of the passengers were milling about the car to get a look at the dead bandits and to thank Stillman for his help. An old woman grabbed him around the neck and kissed his cheek.

Stillman headed back toward his seat, where Fay was standing, looking at him with relief plain in her lovely features. She shook her head slowly and tried a smile as he approached.

The ex-marshal took his young wife gently in his arms, kissed her forehead, and held her to his chest.

"Well, Mrs. Stillman," he said with a sigh, "welcome back to Montana."

4

Bob Andrews and E. L. "Scratch" Lawson galloped their horses southeast from the railroad bed, traversed a thin cottonwood copse, and descended the deep gash of Big Sandy Creek, glancing over their shoulders to see if any of their brethren were following them.

It was too much to hope for, they both knew. They'd deduced from the yelling and gunfire that all three men aboard the train had gone down in a holy hail of lead. That's why they hadn't hung around to be next. Instead they'd released the horses of their compañeros, and lit a shuck.

When their mounts had ascended the opposite bank, choosing a game trail that took the steep grade at an angle, Bob Andrews halted his and slipped out of the saddle.

He handed his reins to Scratch. "I'm gonna take a look and see what's what." He dug in his saddlebags for his spyglass.

Scratch was so riled, his big slab of sun- and wind-burned face was swollen up like he'd been snakebit. His big, bushy black mustache was wet with sweat. "There ain't nobody followin' us. Those boys are dead—I know it. Otherwise, they woulda come a-runnin'! Whoever was back there in that passenger car . . . shit!"

"Yeah, I'll say shit," Bob Andrews said, voice fairly

quaking with emotion. His brother, Howard, had been one of the men in the passenger car when all the shooting had occurred. "Wait till Pa hears about this."

He didn't know what made him feel worse—the death of his little brother, Howard, or the prospect of what his father would do to him and Scratch when he found out Howie was dead and that Bob and Scratch had hightailed it out of there without so much as flinging a single slug.

The eyepiece snugged up against his face, he swept slowly right to left, bringing up the train bed, the cottonwoods beneath it, the dry slough cluttered with cattails, and the open stretch of wheat grass between the slough and the ravine. The train was still there where they'd left it, idling on the tracks under the big blue bowl of prairie sky.

Four men were out inspecting the damaged rails. Training the spyglass on them, Bob recognized the engineer, the fireman, and the conductor. The other man Bob recognized as the one he'd seen through the window of the passenger car, shooting at Howard, Lefty, and Clem—a broad-shouldered, slim-waisted hombre in a crisp, cream, ten-gallon Stetson and a big mustache flecked with gray.

Bob held the glass on the man for a long time, feeling anger burn up through the bile in his stomach. Who was that son of a bitch, anyway? Why in hell did he have to pick today to ride the train?

Bob then aimed the spyglass north, toward the little village of Box Elder—the scattered shacks of which were just over the horizon. Bob thought maybe one or two of the others, if they'd managed to leave the train alive, might have headed that way. But there was nothing more out there than gently undulating swells of blond prairie grass interrupted here and there by a lone cottonwood or a box elder. The windmill of the Gustach ranch rose up in the west, only the idle blades visible above the sod.

Apparently, Scratch had see the men out inspecting the damaged rails. "I say we ride back there and give them the what-for, that's what I say," he said through clenched teeth.

Bob looked at him with contempt. "You sure are brave now! Where the hell were you ten minutes ago? All I saw was your back, galloping away!"

"Well . . . goddamnit . . . all that shootin' . . . it riled me . . . I couldn't think straight. I didn't mean to run."

"Maybe you didn't mean to, but run you sure as hell did!"

"Well, so did you, Bob!"

"Only 'cause I seen you runnin', by god! I figured you must've seen someone else comin' around the other side of the train or something, with a shotgun. . . . What was I supposed to do, stay there and take on that bastard by my lonesome?"

Scratch acquired the air of a chastised child. "It was an honest mistake. Hell, I never robbed a train before."

"Neither did I."

"Leave me alone, Bob."

"Yeah, wait till Pa hears about this. Then we'll see who leaves you alone."

Bob Andrews brought the eyepiece back up and focused the glass on the train, sitting there with black smoke curling from the big funnel-shaped smokestack and sun winking off its fittings and windows. He slid it northward, to where the four men were inspecting the rails. One stood off from the others.

Bob isolated the man, fine-tuning the spyglass. It was the big hombre who'd killed his brother and his friends. The man was holding something up to his face. What the hell? Bob tried to quell his breathing and steady his hands on the spyglass. Finally he saw that the man was holding his own spyglass up to his eye, and was aiming it this way!

Bob swallowed, wanting to run. He kept the spyglass on the man. The man took his left hand off the glass and held it up, waving. Bob couldn't see from this distance, but something told him the man was grinning, as well.

"What is it?" Scratch asked him, seeing the fearful, blanched look on Bob's narrow face.

"Nothin,' " Bob groused, bringing the glass down, reducing it, and scrambling to his feet. "Let's get the hell out of here."

They mounted quickly and rode due east along the creek, then turned around Little Jim Butte in the Two Bear Mountains, and angled south through pine forests and draws teaming with aspens and freshets bubbling from rocky springs. There were squatter cabins here and there, and when they were five miles as the crow flies from the stalled train, Bob had gotten enough pluck back to take a shot at a farm boy cultivating a potato field in Horse Head Hollow.

The boy dropped the plow, and he and the horse broke and ran in opposite directions, the kid screaming at the cabin sitting back in the woods, "It's them! It's them! It's the Andrews gang!"

Bob whooped.

"You crazy sumbitch!"

"Go diddle yourself, Scratch!"

A half hour later they came out on the ridge over-looking the Andrews ranch, if you could call it a ranch. It was as much an outlaw hideout as a ten-cow stock operation, working out of an unpainted, wood frame shack with a tin roof. To the left of the cabin sat a barn abutted on both sides by lean-to sheds and flanked by broken wheels and seats and other wagon parts. The weeds around the barn grew as high as a man's waist.

There were a few rusted implements buried in the weeds around the windmill and water trough, and there were three horses in the peeled log corral. There was no outhouse. Dillon Andrews, the patriarch of the Andrews ranch, did not believe in building shelters over shit holes, when it was just as easy to shit over a deadfall log in the woods. If you had to shit badly enough, you'd shit in the rain, with or without a roof over your head, or use a slops pail inside.

The old man was wrestling and cursing a wagon jack in the yard when he heard the horses in the corral whinny. He looked up from the jack with which he was trying to peel the axle of a dilapidated hay wagon off the hard-packed yard. He aimed his hawkish face with its deep-set mud-brown eyes at his son and E. L. "Scratch" Lawson riding down the ridge, through the brightly colored carpet of balsam root and shooting star.

Bob Andrews was more scared now than he'd been back at the train. He wondered if it might have made more sense to tussle with that rough who'd killed his brother than to return home to explain the situation to his father, who was eyeing him now from the yard, fists on his hips, his characteristically vile gaze tempered only by dark curiosity. He knew something had gone wrong; otherwise, Bob and Scratch and the other three would be riding back together.

"What the hell happened?" the old man barked as Bob and Scratch approached on their hang-headed geldings. Even the horses looked cowed and apprehensive around the old man.

"Trouble, Pa."

"What kinda trouble?"

"Howie and the others . . . they didn't make it."

The old man's face swelled and turned red. He was blinking as though the light was in his eyes, but it was behind him. "Wh—what the hell happened?" he said darkly.

Bob turned to Scratch, who looked down at his saddle horn, working his lips together, cringing against the inevitable onslaught of the old man's awful wrath. Bob turned back to his father.

"There was a shoot-out. They back-shot 'em ridin' away, the cowardly devils. We turned to return fire but there was just too many of 'em—had to be five, six, maybe seven openin' up on us with rifles."

"Five, six, or seven, you say?" Dillon Andrews said, inclining his head and acquiring a skeptical stare. "You scouted that run for the last two weeks, said it looked easy."

Bob shook his head and glanced again at Scratch for help, who offered none. "I know, Pa, but this time some of those passengers was totin' scatterguns and such."

"I thought you said rifles."

"Them, too."

The old man studied the two young men warily. Then, as the death of his youngest boy took hold, he turned away to look at the sandstone ridge poking up east of the ranch, its slopes furry with choke- and juneberry and a smattering of wildflowers.

The cabin door opened and a young blond woman appeared—or girl rather. All of seventeen, she was wearing a white dress with puffy sleeves and two bands of white lace down around the skirt. There was a red ribbon stuck in her hair, above her left ear. She had a hesitant look on her pale, round face, the two blue eyes peering reluctantly at Bob and Scratch.

Bob knew Evelyn, the whore Howie had brought back from Helena to cook and clean and satisfy Howie's masculine desires, had gussied herself up for Howie's return with the loot. Only there wasn't any loot, and there wasn't any Howie.

"What happened?" Evelyn said, standing on the single plank step below the cabin door.

"Howie's dead," Bob told her with a sigh.

The girl swallowed and folded her arms across her bosom. She looked pleadingly at Bob for several seconds. Tears welled in her eyes. Then she turned, fumbled with the doorknob, and disappeared inside the cabin.

"Unsaddle your horses," the old man said tightly, still staring off at the rock formation. His face was dangerously expressionless.

Bob shuttled an ominous look to Scratch, who returned it. Silently they dismounted and led their horses into the barn.

They'd unsaddled the animals, shelved the saddles,

and were filling the troughs with oats when Bob heard something and turned to the open doorway. His father was standing there, silhouetted against the daylight. He was holding a long blacksnake.

"Come here," he snapped.

Scratch peered darkly at Bob from over his horse's back, then turned to walk around behind the gelding. Both horses were munching oats contentedly, swishing their tails. That and flies buzzing around the walls were the only sounds. Bob met Scratch at the rear of his horse, the men's eyes locking significantly before turning to the old man standing in the doorway holding the blacksnake straight down at his side, the long leather whip curling in the dust.

"Now I wanna know what happened, and I wanna hear the truth this time."

"I told you, Pa—"

The old man's hand rose in a blur. The blacksnake curled through the air, catching Bob across the shoulders, tearing his shirt. "Ouch, Pa!"

The horses whinnied and reared against the ropes securing them in their stalls.

The blacksnake careened through the air again, striking Scratch with a sharp crack. Scratch fell back with a yelp, losing his hat and rolling on the hay- and manure-packed floor of the barn. The horses whinnied and kicked the wood partitions. Swallows wheeled from the rafters and fled through the cracks in the log walls.

"You two ran, didn't you? *Didn't* you?"

The blacksnake ripped into Bob again, turning him around and sprawling into a four-by-four roof joist from which bridles and halters hung. "No, Pa! I mean—hell, this hombre in the train, he just started shootin'—and before we knew it, all three of 'em were down. We didn't know what else to do—"

"So you broke and ran!"

Crack!

"No, Pa—I didn't! It was Scratch!"

The snake whistled in the air and cracked against Scratch's back, laying open the man's shirt and undershirt to a bloody strip of skin. "So ya *both* ran!"

"I didn't mean to run, Uncle Dillon—I swear! My horse spooked, and then all of a sudden I was runnin' away and couldn't get him stopped . . . so I just kept goin'!"

"You ran and left my boy and your friends to die!"

Bob turned away when he saw the whip coming toward him again. As it cracked across his back, the old man yelled, "You left your little brother to die on that train!"

For the next five minutes, the blacksnake cracked into each of the bloody, cowering men in turn, one after the other. The horses screamed and kicked their stalls, churning powdery dust and hay. The young men moaned and groaned and begged the old man to stop.

But he wouldn't stop until neither Bob nor Scratch was able to respond to the whipping; they lay semiconscious in bloody, tattered heaps about the hard-packed floor of the barn.

The old man calmly and deliberately hung the blacksnake on a joist, then picked up a bucket and went to the tank at the base of the windmill. He returned a moment later, throwing half the water on Bob, the other half on Scratch. Both men groaned and stirred, sobbing like children.

"Listen to me now!" the old man roared at Bob. "You find whoever it was who killed your brother, and you make him pay. Do you hear me?"

Bob groaned. Scratch was trying feebly to pull himself to his feet, using the roof joist for support. His hands were bloody, as was his back, beneath the torn strips of his shirt.

"Do you hear me? Leave in the morning and don't come home until he's dead. One man, you say—*huh!*" The old man snorted and shook his head with contempt.

Bob spat blood and pushed himself to his knees. "I . . . I hear ya, Pa. We'll get him, Pa. I . . . I swear we will."

Later that night, Bob and Scratch were lying on cots in the barn, sharing a bottle of busthead Bob had hid out there, away from the old man whose weakness for whiskey was notorious. Earlier, Evelyn had come out from the house with a basin of water, rags, and an old sheet torn into strips for bandages to doctor their wounds.

Now they tossed the bottle back and forth, recorking it after each slug. The two empty cots nearby were a ghastly, additional admonition of their cowardice, for they were where Lefty and Clem had slept. Howie had slept with Evelyn and the old man in the house.

Neither man said anything. They lay there in the lantern light, slugging whiskey and growing more and more morose . . . and angry at the son of a bitch who had gotten them into trouble.

They were going to get him, whoever he was. It was the only way they'd be able to look themselves in the mirror again, not to mention face the old man. He was the meanest, most crotchety, evil, hard-hearted bastard either of them had ever known. Still, they wanted nothing more than to please him, and to that end would strive as they had always striven, against the odds, and despite the futility of their efforts. No one—not even Howie, the old man's favorite—had ever totally pleased Dillon Andrews.

The barn door scraped open. Both men tightened and stared anxiously at the entrance. They did not want any more run-ins with the old man. Especially after he'd been drinking, which, since it was nearly nine o'clock, he'd been doing for the past five hours. Sitting in his chair, staring, and drinking.

"Boys." It was Evelyn.

Both men sighed. Bob swallowed the whiskey he'd suspended in his mouth when he'd heard the door, and watched the girl enter the lantern light. She still wore the white dress she'd been wearing for Howie, as well as the ribbon. Her face was puffy from crying. She was holding what appeared to be a wadded up towel.

"Mr. Andrews didn't want me bringin' you nothin' to eat, but I managed to squirrel away a few biscuits after supper. The old man has drunk himself up tighter than an old clock, so I managed to slip away. Here you go. Dig in. It may be all you'll have for a while. He said no breakfast, neither."

"I ain't hungry," Bob said.

"You have to eat something, Mr. Bob."

She always called him Mr. Bob for some reason. She liked to play with words. Scratch was "Atch," Howie was "Mowie," Lefty was "Mr. Right," and Clem was "My Darling Clementine," which had pissed Clem off to no end. "Hello, My Darling Clementine," she'd say, and Howie would howl. Dillon Andrews had been her "Little Cutie Pie" only once. Now he was, without exception, Mr. Andrews—to his face, anyway.

"I told you I don't want nothing," Bob said, taking one of the biscuits and throwing it against the wall. It struck with a thump and hit the floor.

"I'll take one," Scratch said meekly.

He took one of the biscuits from the towel Evelyn held out to him, and bit into it. "You sure can make a biscuit, Miss Evy," Scratch said.

"Thanks, Atch," the girl said with a note of sadness in her voice. She sat down on the foot of Scratch's cot and looked mournfully at Bob.

"I can't believe he's dead, Mr. Bob."

"Well, he is, and that's that."

"The old man's real broken up. He's even cryin' in there. I never seen him cry before. It's scary. Gives me the shivers to see a man like that cry."

"Yeah, the golden boy is dead."

"He scares me. I ain't ashamed to tell you that."

Bob chuffed a mirthless laugh. "Hell, he scares me, too."

Scratch reached for another biscuit, and Evelyn handed him the whole towel.

"I don't know what I'm gonna do with myself now," Evelyn said, looking down at her hands.

"You best go back to where ya came from, I reckon."

"I was wonderin' where you boys was goin'."

"How the hell should we know? I reckon we're going after the sumbitch who shot the golden boy and Lefty and your Darling Clementine."

"Can I go with?"

Bob looked at her. She wasn't a bad-looking girl, and he'd often listened outside the cabin when she and the golden boy were going at it, after the old man had drunk himself into a stupor. Bob thought he wouldn't mind having some of that himself, only Howie hadn't been the sharing type. Bob had never lain with a woman who looked even remotely as good as Evelyn. He felt a sudden interest stirring his loins.

He glanced at Scratch, devouring a biscuit. "I don't know, Atch. What do you think?"

Scratch shrugged, swallowing with some effort. The biscuits had dried out. "Hell, I don't know nothin'." He was still tending the psychological wounds of the beating.

"I'll do your cookin' and cleanin' for ya. Just like I do here," the girl said.

Bob pushed himself up on his cot, rested his head against the log wall. A thin, carnal smile grew on his face. "What else will you do for me?"

The girl looked at her hands again. "Well, I reckon I'll do whatever you want, Mr. Bob . . ."

"You do for me what you did for the golden boy?"

She looked up, tipped her head, and arched an eyebrow. "Well . . . we'd have to see about that, now wouldn't we? A girl doesn't just—"

"A girl just does if she don't want to stay and diddle the old man."

"Why, you're blackmailin' me, Mr. Bob!"

"Yes, I am." Bob grinned broadly. "Show me your titties."

Evelyn looked at him sharply, cheeks blushing.

"That's crude . . . and not in front of Atch!"

"Turn over, Atch."

"Oh, come on, now, you two . . ."

"Turn over, goddamnit, or I'll go tell the old man you been stealin' his liquor!"

"Oh, shit . . . all right." Scratch turned on his side, away from Bob.

Evelyn got up slowly and walked over to the lantern. "Leave it on," Bob said, "and get out of that dress."

She turned to him. "You promise you'll take me with you?"

"You get out of that dress, and give me what you been givin' the golden boy, and it's a definite possibility."

She stood there for a while, whetting Bob's interest. Then slowly, with the air of a girl who had practiced such an operation more than a few times in the past, she slid the dress down her shoulders, revealing the firm, white globes of her young breasts.

Bob's eyes grew wantonly dark and sleepy. He patted the cot beside him, and Evelyn walked slowly toward him, smiling faintly, coquettishly.

Bob swallowed as she sat down, ran the back of his knuckles down her bare arm. "So this is what the golden boy was gettin'."

Then he grabbed her hair and pulled her down.

5

Earlier that evening, after the tracks had been repaired—
a nearly three-hour endeavor involving Stillman, the
train's brakeman, engineer, and a two-man railroad crew
hailed from Box Elder—the train wound around the last
curve into Clantick, sparks mushrooming from the
smokestack and the whistle signaling its approach.

"Well, I'm glad that uneventful little jaunt is over
with," Fay said dryly as she and Stillman jounced to the
train's clattering rhythm, leaning back against the green
velvet cushions.

Stillman glanced out the window. Dark clouds, their
bellies crimson with the sun's dying rays, compressed
the evening glow to a thin bar over the western pastures
relieved here and there by hills and chalky buttes. He
sighed fatefully, thinking back to the robbery he'd
foiled. "Jody wasn't kidding when he said the place was
getting wild."

Fay lifted one of her perfect eyebrows. "Any second
thoughts?"

"A few," Stillman admitted, smoothing his mustache.
He turned his clear blue eyes to his wife. "But on account of you, not me."

The train was slowing now, and the other passengers
rose to gather their bags from the overhead compart-
ments. Their faces still appeared stricken from the bout

with the bandits, and their voices betrayed their relief at the approach of civilization—or what passed for civilization out here.

Fay clutched his wrist. "Ben, you are the only man I have ever loved. You're the only man I *will* ever love. If anything happened to you, I don't know what I would do. But you have to do whatever it is that makes you Ben Stillman, the man I love." She smiled ironically, and shrugged, suppressing a sigh. "And for now I guess that is becoming sheriff of Clantick, Montana Territory."

"I feel like a heel, taking you out of Denver just when you were getting to know so many interesting people."

"My darling, I couldn't be truly happy in Denver, knowing you weren't satisfied with your job. Besides, this is my home, remember? I was beginning to miss my horseback rides in the Two Bears."

The train shuddered to a stop, and Stillman gripped the seat before him. "Fay," he said to his wife, with love in his eyes, "they really did break the mold when they made you."

"You'd better hope so," Fay said with her husky laugh, her English edged a little with the French she'd spoken at her family's ranch near the Yellowstone River until she was twelve years old.

Stillman had met her there, nine years ago, when as a deputy U.S. marshal, he'd gone to Miles City to help the local sheriff with a vigilante problem. Despite the fifteen-year gap in their ages, they'd promptly fallen in love. Stillman asked Fay's father, the indomitable, wealthy Alexander Beaumont, for Fay's hand in marriage. Beaumont granted it, but later changed his mind, privately imploring Stillman not to go through with the ceremony.

Stillman was obviously a career lawman, and what kind of a life could such a man offer Beaumont's beautiful, precocious daughter, who'd been raised on classical French literature and the finest blooded horses in the West?

Stillman had written Fay a letter explaining that his job had called him away and that he'd not be back to the Yellowstone River country . . . that the marriage was off.

He saw her again seven years later, after a bullet in his back had made him retire his badge. She was married to the British heir, Donovan Hobbs, a ruthless, murdering cattle baron who owned a ranch near Clantick. Stillman was on the Hi-Line, unofficially investigating the death of his old hide-hunting friend, Bill Harmon, Jody Harmon's father. He wound up foiling Hobbs's rustling operation, killing the man, and marrying Fay at last.

Now here they were again, where it all had started . . . the second time.

"Shall we?" Stillman said, standing and offering his hand to the exquisitely lovely woman.

When the aisle had cleared, Stillman retrieved Fay's carpetbag, his war bag, and the worn leather sheath containing his Henry rifle from the overhead compartment. Fay took the carpetbag, and Stillman followed her down the aisle and onto the car's platform.

The kerosene lamps outside the station house were lit and attracting moths; the dusk had settled in earnest, blurring edges and drawing shadows out from the roof over the station house platform. Looking around, Stillman saw Jody Harmon searching the cars.

Stillman was about to call to him when he saw Crystal walking down the line of cars, studying the windows and glancing at the disembarking passengers. From this distance, you could have mistaken her for a cowpoke, in her denim jeans, cowhide vest, and flat-brimmed hat. Many cowboys had started growing their hair nearly as long as hers. But there was no mistaking the womanly curves under the garb, or the lovely lines of her fine-boned, Nordic face.

Suddenly she saw Stillman and waved. "Mr. Stillman!" she called. Then to Jody, "They're down here!"

Jody turned and, seeing Stillman, hurried down the line of cars. Crystal wrapped her arms around the lawman's neck and hitched her chin over his big shoulder.

"It's so good to see you again, Mr. Stillman! I'm so glad you came!" She pushed away and looked at him with concerned appraisal. "Are you all right? We heard there was trouble . . ."

Stillman shook his head. "I'm fine. And it's good to see you, too, Crystal." He'd known her for only a few months two years ago, but she'd become like a daughter to him.

Crystal slipped from his arms into Fay's, and Jody stepped up, holding out his hand. "Nice to see you again, Mr. Stillman," he said with a shy smile. "Sorry about your welcoming party, but I told you in my letter it was getting pretty woolly around here."

"You did at that, son," Stillman said, disregarding the boy's hand and engulfing the lad in his arms.

He could tell by the width of the boy's shoulders that he'd put on muscle since Stillman had last seen him.

Jody had been seventeen then, just a boy, though his father's murder had made him grow up fast. Now he stood only an inch or two shorter than Stillman's six-feet-one, and had filled out quite a bit.

Pushing the boy back and holding him at arm's length for inspection, Stillman saw that the kid had become a handsome man, with dark, half-Indian features, blue-green eyes, and a solid jaw beneath a black, round-brimmed hat boasting a snakeskin band. His mother had been a full-blooded Cree.

"You've turned into quite the man," Stillman said admiringly. "Your father would be right proud."

"Thank you, Mr. Stillman. I'd like to think so."

"Bet on it."

Jody tipped his hat brim at Fay. "Pleased to see you again, Mrs. Stillman."

"The pleasure's mine, Jody," Fay said, giving the boy a heartfelt hug. "How've you been?"

"Well, with all that land you gave us, we couldn't have done much better," Jody said.

"Donovan Hobbs gave you that land. He owed it to you for all the trouble he caused around here. After burning your ranch . . ."

"I rebuilt the headquarters, then split up the range and doled out parcels to all the other ranchers he rustled cattle from," Jody told her, feeling a little guilty. She and Mr. Stillman could probably use that land now, to build a house and maybe even run a few beeves on. Jody knew that Fay's father had died penniless, having lost his fortune to several bad winters in the Yellowstone River country. Fay had inherited nothing.

She nodded knowingly. "I had a feeling you might do that."

"The rest we turned back to open range, so we could all graze our beef on it. Seemed like the fairest thing to do."

"I agree." Reading the doubt in Jody's eyes, Fay added sincerely, "Ben and I wouldn't have it any other way, Jody. There's more to life than land and money." Fay's brown eyes widened, and the lights from the lamps danced in them prettily.

"Oh, my god," Crystal breathed.

Stillman glanced around. The conductor, Ted March, and a porter were hauling one of the dead bandits off the train on a stretcher. March looked at Stillman. "We'll lay them out in the back room of the station house, Ben."

"Sounds good, Ted. Tell the coroner I want to know when they've been identified."

"Will do."

To Jody, Stillman said, "You said in your last cable that the city council was meeting tonight."

"They're waiting for you over at the Boston, Mr. Stillman. I've arranged for your luggage to be hauled over by dray."

"What in the hell is the Boston?" Stillman said, incredulous.

Jody smiled. "The Boston is the best hotel in town. Chinese rugs, crystal chandeliers, and everything!"

"I believe those are *Ori-ental* rugs," Crystal whimsically corrected.

"That's where you and Mrs. Stillman will be staying until you can find permanent lodgings," Jody said to

Stillman. "The council members are waiting there to brief you on the situation around here."

Stillman glanced guiltily at Fay, then furled his eyebrows at Jody. "I don't know if I can afford any hotel called the Boston."

"It's all been taken care of by the council, Mr. Stillman," Jody said, relieving Fay of her carpetbag and leading the group around the station house, toward the street and the two-seater buggy waiting by the hitching post, a pair of black fillies in the traces.

"The councilmen worked out a deal with the gentleman who runs the place. He's an old fan of yours, it turns out. Kept up with your career in the newspapers. He's giving the council your room for a third his going rate in return for your permission to call it the Ben Stillman room forever after."

"I'm flattered, but I hardly—"

"Nonsense, Mr. Stillman," Jody interrupted, setting the carpetbag in the buggy. He turned back to Stillman, reaching for the rifle sheath. "Don't you know you're still famous around here?"

Not for long, Stillman thought. Pretty soon I'm going to be about as popular as gout.

6

On his way to the Boston in the sleek, black surrey provided by the hotel, Stillman saw that Clantick had doubled in size in the two years since his last visit. Both sides of First Street, and about three or four cross streets, were lined with many of the log and rickety frame buildings Stillman remembered. But there were at least a dozen two- and three-story brick structures, as well.

He counted no less than seven saloons and gambling parlors and three of what Stillman's veteran eye detected as houses of ill repute—all nestled together down a side street. The shingles suspended over the street on posts declared one simply "Alma's." Another was called "Serena's First Avenue Pleasure Palace." The third shingle read simply "Rooms By the Hour."

Even at the end of the day, the dusty streets were choked with ranch wagons, drays, and spring buggies with long whips jostling up from their holders. Twice Jody had to halt the two matched fillies pulling the buggy, and wait for the traffic to disperse.

Many of the men on the street were obviously businessmen, dressed as they were in bowler hats and broadcloth suits. Many of the women were obviously "respectable," wearing conservative hats and long gowns reaching, even now in summer, from their cameo-bedecked throats to their high-topped, lace-up shoes.

But most of the women on the street were cavorting outside the saloons in skimpy leg- and cleavage-revealing party dresses. And most of the men on the street were range-worn, dust-covered cowboys, who had probably trailed a herd up from Texas or Oklahoma or been uprooted by grangers' plows from the Dakotas or other Territorial lands, like the Cherokee Strip and the Big Pasture.

There were others—clerks, gamblers, drummers, clodhoppers, Indians, Chinese, children of all shapes, sizes, and colors, a few professional men, as well as soldiers from nearby Fort Assiniboine—making one big, frothy concoction of a frontier town, not at all unlike Dodge City and Abilene in their heydays. Just a little farther north, a little farther off the beaten path, a little farther from the reach of the big newspapers.

Stillman saw the danger in it, but he had to admit this colorful, chaotic mob stirred him, awakened something within him that had lain dormant for years. Clantick reminded him of the old days back in Milestown and Glendive, when he and the West were young.

He'd soon have another badge pinned to his chest, just like old times . . .

"Greetings, Mr. Stillman," said a stiff-looking, middle-aged gent at the entrance to the dining room of the Boston Hotel. "I am Bernard McFadden, president of the Stockman's Bank and Trust, and chairman of the Clantick City Council."

Stillman appraised the man's tall, lanky frame, taking in the tailored broadcloth suit and the finest silk shirt money could buy—west of the Mississippi, anyway.

"Mr. McFadden took over the bank after Mr. Anderson died," Jody told Stillman.

Crystal had shown Fay up to her room, where she wanted to freshen up after the long rail journey from Denver.

"A pleasure to meet you, sir," Stillman said, shaking the banker's hand.

"Come in and meet the other council members," McFadden said, turning to the big, linen- and silver-bedecked dining room.

Along the windows to the right, a half dozen men sat around a large, circular table where Stillman could tell from the remaining butter dishes and rumpled and stained tablecloth that a meal had recently been devoured. Four of the men were still working on dessert— German chocolate cake and ice cream, it appeared. All were drinking coffee out of silver pots and bone china.

"I'm afraid when we heard you ran into trouble down the line, we decided to go ahead and eat without you," McFadden explained. "Would've sent a posse, but the cable said you'd taken care of the . . . the . . . situation."

Stillman approached the table, holding his hat in his hands, feeling a little cowed by this passel of boosters giving him the twice-over, most of whom were dressed similarly to McFadden. Well clothed, well fed, well groomed, and not one appearing under thirty years of age. The town had indeed changed in two years. Stillman had expected to find at least one cowboy or granger among the city's powers-that-be.

"Well, sometimes we get lucky and sometimes we don't," Stillman said with a sigh, taking the chair McFadden indicated. Jody sat next to him.

"Jody's already eaten, but I'll order you a plate, Mr. Stillman."

Stillman waved the offer. "I'll eat later with my wife. You gentleman go ahead with your dessert. I'll partake of the coffee, however. Looks good and smells even better."

"I believe it's from Africa," McFadden said, turning Stillman's cup right-side-up and pouring the rich, aromatic brew.

McFadden went around the table, introducing Stillman to the county judge and all the councilmen, including the owner of a freighting company, a lawyer, a barber, a Lutheran minister, and a co-owner of the Pepin/Baldwin Mercantile. Leroy Pepin pulled a half-smoked stogey from his mouth and asked, "How many bandits were there, Mr. Stillman?"

"Five as far as I could tell. I took care of the three on the train, but there were two outside holding the horses. They got away. I'll go after them tomorrow, after I'm sworn in and everything's official."

"You dispatched all those men yourself?" McFadden asked Stillman with an arched eyebrow.

"Didn't have a choice," Stillman said. "They were starting to get rough with the passengers. I saw an opportunity and took it."

"Didn't I tell you he was the right man for the job?" Jody said to the table in general. His expression belied the relief he felt.

His initial impulse to convince the Clantick City Council to offer Stillman the sheriff's job had later been tempered with doubt. Stillman had solved the rustling problem two years ago, and had killed Donovan Hobbs in a gun battle. But could the forty-six-year-old lawman clean up the whole, burgeoning town of Clantick, with all its contesting factions? The incident on the train gave Jody the answer he'd been searching for.

McFadden worried a toothpick between his narrow lips. "Yes . . . well, I certainly hope you gave them an opportunity to surrender, Mr. Stillman. We do indeed need law and order around here, but what we do not need is the kind of roughshod justice they've been seeing down around Virginia City of late."

Stillman looked at the man, his face flushing beneath his tan. "Are you suggesting I might have *murdered* those men, Mr. McFadden?"

Oscar Peterson, the Lutheran minister—a bald little man with a bushy, gray, upswept mustache—raised a placating hand. "I don't think that's what Bernard means at all, Mr. Stillman. We're just a little wary—that's all— of bringing in someone who may compound our problems. It's happened before, in other towns on the Hi-Line. The council brings in a man who becomes more of a problem than the one he was brought in to solve."

"Oh, hogwater, Oscar!" piped up the owner of the mercantile, Leroy Pepin. "It's not like we're bringing in some West Texas gunslick to form firing squads and bring marshal law to Dodge. You know Stillman's record as well as the rest of us. He's a respected lawman, for heaven's sake. Would you rather hire another Ralph Merchant, and all he does is hunt in the mountains and carouse in the roadhouses?"

"Merchant is not here to defend himself," the minister admonished Pepin.

"No, he's not. And the reason he's not is someone

murdered him." Pepin pounded the table for emphasis.
"And that person is still at large!"

"Pepin's right—it's time we got tough," Edgar
Tempe, the barber, cut in. "It's gotten so bad out there,
I can't let my wife and daughter walk over to Pepin's
mercantile for a spool of thread at high noon!" He turned
to Jody. "Lad, tell Mr. Stillman about our friend, Daryl
Bruner, gunned down in the street by an unruly lot of
drunken drovers!"

"I mentioned it in my letter to you, Mr. Stillman,"
Jody said, and went on to tell Stillman the whole story.
When he was through, his voice was tight and his eyes
were hard.

"Crystal saw it all?" Stillman asked when the young
man was finished.

"The whole thing—and got her face smacked to
boot!"

"And you know for certain the killer's name and who
he works for?"

"Rafe Paul. He's ramrod for Norman Billingsley. Billingsley runs cattle on about ten thousand acres north of
the Milk."

For the first time the county judge, Charles Humperdink, spoke up, raising a long, wrinkled hand. "We must
remember what Norman Billingsley has done for Clantick in the year and a half he's been here." Humperdink
wore a charcoal suit, waistcoat, and a black foulard cra-
vat. His face was like a slab of red beef that had been
scarred by a sharp knife. It was a startling contrast to
his silver beard, which lent a grandfatherly touch.

"His men shoot up the town every Saturday night,
Judge," Jody pointed out, respectfully.

The judge raised his hand again. "And a few of the more reckless have spent time in jail for it. I hasten to add that the Saturday-night hoorahing is not limited to Norman's men." He turned his eyes to Leroy Pepin. "But I'd bet those men, including Norman himself, account for at least fifty percent of all the business you do over at the mercantile—isn't that right, Leroy? Please correct me if I'm wrong."

"I just don't like what he's done to the town, Judge," Pepin said mildly.

The judge snorted mirthlessly. "Without men like Norman, we wouldn't *have* a town."

There was a pause as most of the men contemplated their coffee cups. Stillman looked at the judge, whose eyes met McFadden's, at the other end of the table. There seemed to be two factions here—the county judge and the banker on one side, and the rest of the city council on the other. Curious.

Stillman cleared his throat and said to Jody, "Tomorrow I'll write out a warrant and pick up this Rafe Paul for questioning." He glanced at the judge, gauging the man's reaction. "I'm sure the judge will sign it, since there seems to be legal grounds for suspicion of murder."

The judge stared at him expressionless, slowly turning a butter knife in two gnarled fingers.

"That might be easier said than done, Stillman," Oscar Peterson warned. "Billingsley might not be any more willing to turn Paul over to you than Paul would be willing to go. And he has at least twelve men working for him. Most or all are known gunmen. Like Jody said, they come into town every Saturday night and shoot up at least one saloon, sometimes two."

The lawyer, Dwight Utley, turned to Stillman. "Which brings us to the topic of hiring a deputy."

"I've got a man on the way," Stillman said. "Should be on the train tomorrow. A good man. You'll like him."

"Well . . . good," McFadden said, looking around for concurrence. The others nodded, as well.

The freighter, Kendall St. John, swallowed a slug of coffee and said, "You've got your work cut out for you, Mr. Stillman. You've got Billingsley's crew to worry about, those damn train bandits, and the trouble all these damn drifters keep bringin' to town—cuttin' up pleasure girls and breaking into the homes of our citizens."

"Wanted men use the Hi-Line for a refuge," Peterson said darkly, shaking his bald head.

"And I guess you heard us mention Ralph Merchant," Utley interjected. "His body was found hanging from a cottonwood tree in a creek bottom a month ago—two days after he'd gone out to the Billingsley ranch to arrest Rafe Paul—which Billingsley had talked him out of doing, by the way."

Bernard McFadden sighed with disgust and tossed his napkin on his dessert plate, where his cake and melted ice cream remained, untouched. "We don't know he'd gone out to the Billingsley ranch, Mr. Utley. No one knows that for sure."

"He told his lady friend he was going hunting with some of Billingsley's men, and—"

"Hearsay," the judge intervened.

The attorney scowled. He turned back to Stillman. "The sheriff who preceded Merchant was murdered, as well. Tied to a cot in one of his own cells, and stabbed."

Stillman sipped his coffee, his eyes acquiring a grave cast. "I see."

Peterson said, "I want you to understand, Mr. Stillman, that we are in a critical situation here. If Clantick is going to continue to grow, then we must have law and order. Otherwise, the town will die, and we all might as well go back where we came from. But our wanting to have the town cleaned up is not an excuse for gunplay."

Stillman set his cup down and cast the preacher a direct look. "I'll tell you this, Mr. Peterson. I've been a lawman off and on for twenty years, and if I've learned one thing, it's that you don't kowtow to criminals. You don't show weakness. And you make no exceptions to the rules you've spelled out loud and clear for all to hear. If you do, you might as well paint a target on your back and turn around . . . and give your town back to the devil.

"Now, I'm going to lay out a set of rules for the saloons and the whorehouses to follow by way of quieting down the business district. And I'll bring those two train bandits to justice, just as I'll bring in this Rafe What's-His-Name—if I have to bring in this Billingsley character tied to the same horse." He turned to the judge. "I'm sure you'll back me up, Judge, because that's the law." He sat back in his chair and alternated a study between the judge and McFadden. When he spoke, his voice was slow and even. "Take it, or send me back on the train."

Silence.

The council members studied each other weightily.

Finally, McFadden sighed, flushing a little, and turned to Stillman with a stiff smile. "Well—welcome to Clantick, Sheriff." He shook Stillman's hand. "Oscar, shall we swear the new sheriff in?"

The swearing in took only a minute. McFadden offered Stillman the sheriff's badge. Stillman pinned the star on his shirt and turned to Jody. "Well, young man, shall we go find our women and take a little tour of the town?"

As he and Jody turned to leave, McFadden called from the table. "Oh, Mr. Stillman . . . who's this deputy you're bringing in?"

Stillman stopped and turned around. "Name's McMannigle. Leon McMannigle."

Jody stopped and turned to Stillman abruptly, his eyes glazed with surprise.

Ignoring him, Stillman smiled at McFadden. "A good man, McMannigle. You'll like him."

7

Stillman woke at the first smear of dawn in the sky beyond his open window, through which he could hear the singing of birds and little else. The town was still asleep. He lay there with Fay curled up naked against him, deep in slumber, and stared at the ceiling.

Today would be his first day behind a badge since he'd retired as deputy U.S. marshal five years ago, and he was hesitant. He knew he still had the right instincts for the job—his quick, precise shooting on the train had told him that—and he and Fay had decided together that his injured back should not pin him to a rocker for the rest of his days. He needed to do what he did best, catch criminals and keep the peace, or he might as well be dead.

But what would happen to Fay if anything should go wrong? It was his primary worry, and it led to one more. Would such worry make him hesitate when the chips were down, cloud his focus, cause him to think rather than react, and get him killed?

The West was no place for a lovely woman alone, even one with as much sand as Alexander Beaumont's precocious daughter. She could maybe open a clothing store or a café, but first she'd need capital, and God knows . . .

Fay stirred. She turned her head on the pillow, a rumpled mass of black hair washing over her face. She swept it away with her hand. "What time is it?" she said in a sleep-husky voice.

Stillman picked his watch off the bedside table and opened it. "Five."

"Awake already?"

Stillman shrugged. He glanced at her and smiled. He lifted a hand and ran his fingers thoughtfully through her hair.

Fay knew he was troubled, and she suspected she was the cause. He'd never been both married and a lawman before now. She knew he loved her, but she also knew that love for a frontier lawman was an unwieldy sort of thing, sort of like trying to run a race with irons on your ankles.

She meant to make it as easy for him as possible, which meant talking about it only when he initiated the conversation. Men were different from women in that way; women dealt with problems by talking them out, dragging the monster out from under the bed, so to speak, and giving it a good whack on the head. Men tended their problems in silence, by nature reluctant to trouble those they loved. Sometimes it was best to leave them to their silence or to distract them subtly, with good food, say, or with love . . .

Fay reached up and put her hand on his big, handsome face, brushing his mustache with her thumb. "Let's make love," she said.

He formed an expression of mock horror. "Mrs. Stillman, it's five o'clock in the morning!"

"Maybe this will change your mind," she said, flinging off the covers with a single sweep of her arm. She lay deliciously revealed on her side, resting her head in her hand, regarding him with a dusky smile.

Stillman's expression grew serious as he ran his eyes from the tresses of hair spilling across her shoulders and slender back, down the grade of her curving spine to the womanly upthrust of her splendid buttocks. Her willowy thighs and coltish legs, right to her china-white feet, were long and slender as the rest of her, perfect. Bringing his gaze back slowly the way it had come, he took a detour across her shoulder to her breasts. The full, milky-white orbs brushed the sheets, the nipples coming erect under the passion of his gaze.

Her voice, just above a whisper: "Do you like what you see, Mr. Stillman?"

"I know I've said it before, but I'll say it again," he breathed. "They really did break the mold after they poured you!"

Smiling up at him, Fay slid her eyes down his broad, muscular chest, across the hard, knotted sinew belts of his taut belly, and down to his full, elongated hardness, bobbing slightly as it throbbed. She took it in her hand and worked on it gently at first, then more firmly, until finally she stopped and climbed on top of him, straddling him, her long hair falling down around her face and pooling on his chest.

He groaned with pleasure as she worked, lifting her hands and running them through the thick salt-and-pepper hair that brushed his neck, pressing her ankles tightly to his calves—grinding into him, warding off his demons, riding into bliss . . .

•   •   •

It was six-fifteen before Stillman finally gave Fay a parting kiss, dressed, and left the lovely lady drowsing back to sleep in the twisted sheets, her cheeks flushed from love.

Stillman swept back his hair, arranged his carefully brushed Stetson on his head, slipped his Henry rifle from its sheath, and walked downstairs. The dining room was closed, so he made his way across the dark lobby in which the night clerk drowsed in an easy chair by the window, an illustrated newspaper open on his lap.

Stillman stood before the heavyset man and cleared his throat. The man's head jerked up from his chest. He opened his eyes, blinking, the paper sliding from his lap.

"Anywhere I can get a bath at this hour?" Stillman asked him.

The man squinted at the clock above the fireplace mantel.

"It's six-thirty," Stillman said.

"Well . . . Albright on Second Avenue, goin' north. He might be up and about . . . this ungodly goddamn hour," the man grumbled.

"Much obliged," Stillman said, tossing the man a nickel which he did not catch.

"Hey, you're the new sheriff, aren't you?" the man asked as Stillman moved to the door.

Stillman turned. "That's right."

"Ben Stillman?"

The lawman nodded.

"Heard about you, but . . . hell, I thought you was dead . . . several years back. A whore shot you down in Virginia City . . ."

"Ah, shit," Stillman growled, "not again." It wasn't

the first time he'd been mistaken for dead.

He let the door close behind him, descended the wide wooden steps of the veranda, and headed west up the silent street, the tips of the false fronts just now catching the first rays of the rising sun.

He found Albright's bathhouse just off Front Street on Second Avenue—a long, narrow building of milled lumber wedged in between Greggson's Tinware and Hardware and the Clantick Apothecary. A calico cat sat on the loafer's bench below the plate-glass window, a half-eaten mouse between its paws.

Stillman went in, found a kid of about thirteen or fourteen stoking the fires in the two stoves, and asked if he was too early for a bath. The kid shrugged, mumbled several sentences in halting, German-inflected English, then directed Stillman to a tub, beside which a plank bench sat below several clothes pegs.

"How much?" Stillman asked the boy, a scrawny youth with soft, fair skin and a cowlick.

"Feefty cints."

"That'll work."

The kid went away while Stillman undressed, and returned with two milk pails of steaming water. He commenced filling the tub, finally topping off the six or so gallons of hot water with two cold. Stillman tested the water with a toe, winced, and climbed slowly in, sighing as the hot water inched up his body.

By the time he was finished with his bath and had dressed, it was a quarter to seven. He combed his hair and walked up the street to see if Sam Wah was still in business.

The Chinaman's restaurant sat where Stillman had

found it two years ago. Sam Wah was serving two drovers before the window when Stillman walked in. Turning
from the drovers, Wah saw Stillman. He stared thoughtfully at the lawman for a long moment. Then his round
face with its Fu Manchu mustache broadened in a grin.

"Ah, Meestor Steelman—ah . . . I heard about you return to Clanteek. Ah, wonderful!" The Chinaman gestured to a stool before the counter. "Come, come, sit
down!"

"Thanks, Sam. Don't mind if I do."

When Stillman had given the restaurant proprietor his
order, Wah turned and disappeared in the kitchen. Several minutes later he brought out a cup of steaming black
coffee and a plate of side pork, scrambled eggs, and
flapjacks. He returned to the kitchen and reappeared a
moment later with a small dish of ruby red chokecherry
syrup, slightly steaming.

"Sam, you must be the best damn cook in the Territory!" Stillman exclaimed, admiring the food before
him.

"Mr. Steelman—you must be best judge! Ha-ha!" The
Chinaman laughed as he turned and headed back to the
kitchen.

As Stillman ate, he was aware of the two drovers
seated before the window. They'd been talking when
Stillman had walked in but had lapsed into conspicuous
silence. Stillman glanced at them over his shoulder. The
man facing him rolled his eyes Stillman's way, making
brief eye contact. Then he turned back to his partner
with a meaningful look.

Dropping his eyes, Stillman saw that both men were

wearing revolvers in oiled holsters tied low on their
thighs.

Sam Wah appeared from the kitchen with his coffeepot. He refilled Stillman's cup, smiling broadly, turned,
and walked over to the drovers' table. As he filled their
cups, the Chinaman's smile faded without a trace. He
turned silent and apprehensive. On his way back to the
kitchen, he gave Stillman a wary look, and disappeared.

Five minutes later, the drovers dropped coins on the
table, and scraped back their chairs as they rose to leave.

Finished with his meal, Stillman swung around on his
stool. "Good mornin'," he said heartily, fashioning a benevolent smile.

Standing, the men stopped and turned to him. "Is it?"
one of them said with a faint smirk pulling at the corners
of his mouth. He was tall and sloppy, narrow-shouldered,
pot-bellied, and wide-hipped. His face was broad and
fleshy, his brown hair stiff and unwashed. His eyes were
cunning and mean.

Stillman stood and offered his hand. "I'm Ben Stillman, the new sheriff of Clantick. Just thought I'd intro-
duce myself. Got into town only last night and haven't
had a chance to get acquainted with many of the citizens."

The man did not shake his hand. Stillman smiled anyway, wanting to seem as nonthreatening as possible. You
didn't get information from men who felt threatened.
Stillman had a feeling these two, with their prominently
displayed sidearms, worked for Norman Billingsley, and
he wanted to find out for sure.

The first man folded his arms over his chest, glancing
at his partner. "I'm . . . I'm Steve Smith," the man said,

the fledgling smirk pulling again at his lips.

Stillman's smile lost some of its luster. He said, "Hi, Steve. And you're?"

The other man was shorter, younger, with a broad nose, a mop of kinky black hair, and olive skin, as though there might have been some Negro and possibly Indian blood back in the family woodpile. He glanced at Smith and smiled. "Why, I'm William Bonny." He shook Stillman's hand, his strange hazel eyes flashing mockery.

"Hi, Bill, pleased to make your acquaintance," Stillman said, not missing a beat. "Say, where you boys from, anyway?"

"Here and there," Smith said cautiously.

"You wranglin' for someone hereabouts?"

"Hereabouts," Billy Bonny said.

"Who might that be, if you don't mind my askin'? Like I said, I'm new to town, and I'm trying to get acquainted."

Smith glanced at Bonny and shrugged. "We run cattle for Mr. Billingsley, up north of town."

"This is Norman Billingsley we're talkin' about?"

"That's right," Smith said.

"Would you give him a message from me?"

Smith frowned. He glanced at Billy Bonny. "Message?"

Stillman suddenly transformed from Mr. Easygoing, Aw-Shucks Sheriff of Clantick to Mr. No-Nonsense Ass-Kicker, his voice taut as Glidden wire. "Tell him that I'm lookin' for one of his drovers named Rafe for the murder of Daryl Bruner. He can either turn Rafe in himself, or I can ride out there and arrest him. But if I

have to ride out there and arrest Rafe, I'm gonna arrest
Billingsley, too, for harboring a fugitive. He has two
days." Stillman stared levelly at Smith.

Smith slid his wary gaze to his partner. He turned
back to Stillman, an angry, mean look forming on his
blunt face. Stillman sensed the punch coming a full second before Smith snapped his arm back and brought his
closed fist forward in a blur.

The lawman raised his right forearm, deflecting the
blow, and smashed a powerful left hook into the side of
Smith's face, making a cracking sound, causing blood
to spurt from the nose that was suddenly lying flat
against the drover's cheek. The blood hit Billy Bonny
in the chest.

Smith gave an "Ugh!" and dropped to a knee.

Billy Bonny swung his startled gaze from his partner
to Stillman, his hand going automatically to the revolver
on his hip.

"Uh-uh," Stillman cautioned, snugging the barrel of
his .44 against the cowboy's forehead, freezing the man.

Out of the corner of his eye, Stillman saw Smith, still
on one knee and red-faced with rage, go for his own
tied-down Colt. He'd just gotten it out of his holster
when Stillman kicked it out of his hand, and it clattered
under a table.

"Why, you son of a *bitch*!" Smith shouted, springing
off his knee and bolting toward Stillman.

Keeping the business end of his Colt planted between
the eyes of Billy Bonny, Stillman used his other hand
to bring a chair up. He thrust it, legs extended, into
Smith. Smith stumbled back with the force of the blow,
yelling curses, and then fell through the plate-glass win-

dow with a terrific roar of shattering glass.

Smith had no sooner landed on the boardwalk than Stillman relieved Billy Bonny, staring at the space Smith had vacated, of his Colt 45. "Outside!" he ordered the dark-skinned drover.

Bonny turned and headed out the door, raising his hands above his head. Stillman pushed him into the street and backed him against a tie rail where the cowboys' startled horses stood straining against their tethers and bewilderedly eyeing Smith, who lay on the boardwalk in a carpet of broken glass. Sam Wah appeared in the broken window, staring awestruck at the prone, raging drover before him.

"You had enough, or do you want me to haul you over to the hoosegow?" Stillman asked Smith. "I haven't seen the inside of the place yet, and I'm just bitin' at the bit to try out one of the cells."

Smith lay on his back, breathing like a fish out of water, aiming his enraged eyes at Stillman. He'd stopped yelling and cursing and appeared to be taking mute stock of the damage he'd incurred. His nose was a wide, bloody spot on his face. One of the horses dropped its neck over the tie rail to inspect the blood. Catching a whiff, it jerked away.

"Ya . . . ya broke my nose, ya son of a bitch."

"You didn't answer my question."

Smith was probing his nose gingerly with his fingers. "I've had enough . . . for now."

Stillman turned to Bonny. "How 'bout you?"

The man looked from Smith to Stillman. He shrugged. "I reckon . . . like Claude—I mean Smith—says. For now."

"Why don't you help ol' Claude onto his horse, and get the hell out of here. Deliver my message to Billingsley. You remember what it was?"

"I remember what it was," Bonny carped, helping his partner to his feet.

"That son of a bitch smashed my nose flat against my face," Smith said. "It's got to be set."

"You can take him over to the doctor's office on your way out of town," Stillman told Bonny. "I'll hold onto your sidearms for safekeeping. You can pick them up on your next trip to town—as long as you're real friendly and ask me nice."

When Bonny and Smith had mounted their horses— an awkward proposition for Smith, who had to keep his hand on his nose to deter the nearly steady flow of blood down his face and onto his chest—Stillman turned to Sam Wah. The restaurant proprietor was still standing in the broken window, considering the glass and blood on the boardwalk.

"Sorry about the window, Sam," Stillman said.

Wah lifted his eyes to the new sheriff and smiled. "You . . . keek ass real good, Meestor Steelman." Wah stepped through the window, onto the boardwalk, and shook Stillman's hand. "And they need it bad, those two. Very bad."

Stillman considered the Chinaman bemusedly, nodding faintly. "I take it they're regulars here?"

"Very bad, very bad, those two. They make ol' Sam a nervous Chineese . . . pointing their guns around . . . scare other customers. Very bad."

"Well, maybe they'll think twice about brandishing bad manners next time they're in town," Stillman said.

"You can send the bill for the window over to the chairman of the city council. He'll take care of it. Much obliged for breakfast, Sam. Be seein' you . . . rather often, I suspect."

Stillman flipped the man a coin, touched his hat brim, and started down the boardwalk.

"Good luck, Meestor Stillman," the Chinaman called in his husky singsong. "Welcome back to Clanteeck."

8

Stillman rented a buckboard wagon and two chestnut geldings at Auld's Livery, on the western edge of town, and got directions to the undertaker's. The geldings weren't the best draft animals in Auld's stable, but they were relatively cheap. Stillman didn't want to antagonize the city council any more than he already had, or would, when they received the note for Sam Wah's broken window.

The undertaker's red frame house sat under a cottonwood tree not far from the livery barn, up a hill on the way out of town. A ravine dropped away to the west of the place, through which a dry wash snaked whitely. A man Stillman took for the undertaker, Clyde Evans, who doubled as a doctor, was climbing out of the ravine as Stillman clattered up on the wagon. Evans was carrying a pail of water.

Stillman bid him good morning and the doctor bid the same, though much less heartily.

"My goddamn well went dry," the doctor groused, indicating the water bucket. He was a short, stocky man with a thick shock of red hair and a magnificent handlebar mustache. He wore a tattered old vest over a threadbare pinstripe shirt. His derby hat was frayed around the curled brim. "Have to haul water up from the well in the goddamn wash. You come for those out-laws?"

"I did."

"What are you going to do with them?"

"Take them back where they came from. I figure I'll run into someone who knows."

Evans shrugged. "I know. They're part of Dillon An-drews's gang. He runs a ranch out in the Two Bears."

"You don't say," Stillman said thoughtfully.

"Just said so, didn't I?"

Stillman inspected the doctor tentatively. "Did I catch you at a bad time?"

"Any time is a bad time for me. I have an ulcer the size of a grapefruit and too goddamn many patients who can't pay their bills with anything but garden greens or chickens. You know how tired I am of chicken and Swiss chard?"

Stillman shrugged. "I'll bet you're regular."

The doctor inspected Stillman acidly, squinting one eye. Finally his shoulders drooped and a smile broke on his face. He dropped his chin and wagged his head. Starting for the house, he said, "So you're Stillman, eh? Our latest savior."

"I'd like to think I'm the *last* one," Stillman replied as he set the wagon brake, wrapped the reins around the brake handle, and climbed to the ground.

"So did the last two, and you know what happened to them," the doctor said over his shoulder. "Got time for a cup of coffee?"

"Always."

The house was small, barren, and messy, with only a handful of pictures on the papered walls. The doctor was obviously a bachelor. His parlor did service as a waiting room, as bespoke the four ladderback chairs, several magazines and newspapers on a low table, and a spittoon. He waved Stillman into the tiny kitchen, where a coffeepot gurgled on the range.

"Throw those catalogs on the floor and have a seat. I occasionally have a woman in to clean for me, but the last one got herself hitched. I get around feeling any embarrassment for my sloth by not entertaining. You don't look especially persnickety, however, so you're welcome to have a seat."

"You're not married, I take it," Stillman remarked as he set a pile of medical catalogs and various other papers on the floor.

"Not hardly," the doctor said with a snort. He filled a cup from the pot and set it before Stillman. Returning to the range, he filled another cup, and sat across from the lawman. "Never have, never will. I go it alone and take my pleasure downtown. For the life of me, I'll never understand why a man marries when he can get his milk for free in one of our glorious flopbarns off First."

"You know, you have a point," Stillman quipped.

"He can return to the peace and quiet of his castle, and belch and fart and cuss to his heart's content." Evans produced a bottle from the floor by his chair and offered it to Stillman. "Red eye?"

"No, thanks."

"And here I took you for a drinking man."

"I was," Stillman said gloomily.

"After you took the bullet?"

"Heard about that, did you?"

Evans shrugged as he added a splash of whiskey to his coffee. "Who didn't? You're famous, Stillman. Not famous enough for me to clean house for you, but famous just the same. I was doctorin' down in Bannock when it happened. Read about it in the newspaper, heard about it in the saloons."

"Why'd you leave Bannock to come here?"

The doctor straightened in his chair and sighed, staring across the room. "I was, shall we say, entertaining a married man's wife. He found out about it and gave me two options, the second of which I took with only the clothes on my back and my medical bag." He grinned.

"Was she worth it?"

"I'd plunder the lady again in a Dutch minute."

"You enjoy living dangerously, Doctor."

"It's the only way," Evans said, raising his cup in a cheer. Blowing on the hot brew, he drank.

"You're from the East?"

Evans nodded. "Maryland. I went to Harvard, like every good son of my father, and interned in Philadelphia. A wild hair up my young ass sent me out West. My father and two brothers are all doctors. They practice in Manhattan and think I'm deranged—though of course they've always thought that. Give them the city life and private clubs, balls at the Waldorf, mistresses with summer homes in the Adirondacks. Give me a good cow town teaming with cowboys and plump whores and"— he looked at Stillman—"sheriffs with bullets riding precariously close to their spines." With a smile he lifted his cup again. "Cheers."

Stillman picked up one of the books from the two

piles on the table, and ran his finger down the spine. *"Love's Labors Lost."*

Evans shrugged. "I wanted to be an English professor, but my father wouldn't hear of it." His eyes lowered thoughtfully to the table, a weary cast fermenting in them. Evans raised his face again to Stillman, fashioning his customary look of wry humor. "What made you decide to come to this hell hole?"

Stillman shrugged. "Jody Harmon asked me. His father was a friend of mine."

"Yes . . . I heard he was killed. . . ." The doctor narrowed his eyes warily, leaving the sentence incomplete.

"By Crystal's father, that's right," Stillman said. "Ugliest situation I ever ran across. Her father didn't like Bill 'cause he'd married an Indian woman. Then when Jody started dating Crystal, well, the old coot went nuts. He didn't think a half-breed was good enough for his daughter."

"He didn't know Jody, then, did he?" Evans said. "That boy's about the most standup man you'll find around here."

"Johnson was bedeviled by drink," Stillman explained, looking thoughtfully off. "He'd been at Beecher Island when the Indians attacked. Was one of the few survivors. Nothing in the world looked right to him after that."

"Those two—Jody and Crystal—had a pretty rocky start."

"Yeah, but they're in love," Stillman said. "That's all it takes."

"You speak from experience?"

Stillman shrugged, flushing a little with embarrassment. Love wasn't something he felt comfortable talking about with other men. "You should give it a shot," he said, in spite of himself.

The doctor laughed cynically and shook his head. Finally, he looked at Stillman and changed the subject. "You ever tame a town before?"

"A few."

"Not like this one, I bet."

"What's different about this one?"

"I've never seen such a hodgepodge of people in my whole Western life—and I've been around. Indians, soldiers, Chinamen, farmers, gunslingers, Germans . . . Easterners—you name 'em, we got 'em. And the ones who'll shoot you in the back aren't necessarily the ones you'd expect."

"I've considerable experience in that department."

Evans leaned over the table and regarded Stillman seriously. "Those two sheriffs who were killed. Well, only one of 'em was killed by crazy cowboys."

"Which one?"

"The first."

"What happened to Ralph Merchant?"

"You tell me. But the last time he was seen alive it was in the company of his hunting companion, Bernard McFadden, and several of McFadden's men."

"You don't say?"

"Just said so, didn't I?" Evans got up and retrieved the coffee cup, filling Stillman's cup before topping off his own. Stillman was considering what the man had just said as Evans returned from the range and added another splash of whiskey to his coffee.

"Why would McFadden want Merchant dead?"

Evans shook his head. His eyes were getting rheumy from drink. "Your guess is as good as mine. I don't know. But I saw those two men together just too goddamn often, and it didn't fit. You've never seen a more incongruous pair. Merchant was a goddamn hillbilly from Arkansas. McFadden is an Eastern-bred money man. Hell, his silver spoon takes twice as long to polish as mine!"

Stillman sipped his coffee and ran a hand across his freshly scraped jaw. "You don't say?" he mumbled to himself.

"Just said so, didn't I?" the doctor said with an eager grin, stretching his neck over the table, eyes bright with drink. He had the air of a scandal-loving housewife.

"You're enjoying this, aren't you?" Stillman groused at him.

Evans's grin lost none of its luster. "It's more entertaining than a goddamn illustrated newspaper." He picked up a book from the stack beside him. "It's pure Shakespeare!"

Scowling, Stillman finished his coffee and slid back his chair. "Come on, Professor," he said. "Show me to those bodies so I can get a move on."

The three outlaws had been laid out in the doctor's barn, on makeshift cots, and covered with a rat-chewed tarp. When Evans and Stillman had loaded them into the buckboard and Evans had drawn Stillman a detailed map to the Andrews ranch in the Two Bears, Stillman climbed into the seat and untied the reins from the brake handle.

"Thanks for the coffee," he said, jerking the reins against the geldings' backs.

"Anytime, Sheriff," the doctor called. "And hey—be careful out there. There's some obvious badasses in them thar hills, but they're not the only ones—"

"I know, I know," Stillman said, not turning around to regard the doctor looking after him. "The only ones who'll shoot you in the back."

Stillman followed a creekside trail south out of Clantick, winding through the countryside toward the pine-clad Two Bear Mountains looming darkly ahead of him.

The day was heating up, and he'd ridden only a mile beyond the town's last outlying tar paper shack when he removed his corduroy coat and laid it beside him on the seat, then scrubbed the sweat from his forehead with his handkerchief.

Rolling his sleeves up his arms, he considered what Doc Evans had told him about the town, especially about the possibility of Bernard McFadden being responsible for Ralph Merchant's murder. Why would the president of the city council want the sheriff dead?

The only answer—if there was an answer, and the whole thing wasn't the zealous workings of Doc Evans's romantic, alcoholic imagination—would have to be that McFadden was involved in something criminal, and Merchant had found out about it. Or maybe he'd already known about it and had become somehow dangerous.

How? Why? And how exactly was Merchant killed? Stillman had heard the man had been lynched north of town, but he wanted to know more. It was the only way he'd be able to know if the doctor had some basis for his suspicions.

When Stillman was resting the horses in the shade of

a winding mountain lane, buffered on both sides by aspens and pines, he considered the good doctor. The man was a cynic, for sure, and apparently a lech, but Stillman had found himself warming to the man.

He knew from previous relationships that such men conjured crusty facades to camouflage innate sensitivities, and that a plucky cynicism was their only way of dealing with life, which, for whatever reason, weighed heavy. They were congenital outsiders who outwardly hated "insiders" with a religious zeal while coveting the security and comfortable acceptance of the herd.

Stillman understood such men because, to a lesser extent, he was such a man himself. Fay and work kept him from oblivion. Clucking to the geldings to get them started again, he thought that he had made an interesting, albeit troubled, friend, in Clyde Evans, and he anticipated speaking with the man again soon.

It was nearly noon, the sun straight up and intense, the temperature nearly ninety, when Stillman came to a trail forking left off the main two-track. Stillman consulted the map Evans had drawn in pencil on a page torn from a ledger book. Moistening his lips with his tongue, he wiped sweat from his brow and glanced at the shaley dike poking up on his right, and the notched ridge ahead of him. Red-winged blackbirds were cackling in a spring wash just down the grade from where Stillman sat the wagon.

This had to be the place. He refolded the map, stuck it in his coat with his tobacco makings, and reached for the Henry rifle, which he'd wrapped in an oiled sheepskin in the box. He checked the loads of the prized gun, which boasted a gold-plated receiver and a pearl bull's head set in the stock—a present from the late Johnny Dawson, Marshal of Dakota Territory.

He jacked the lever, throwing a shell into the chamber, then let the hammer down to half cock and stood the rifle between his knees. Checking the Army .44 he wore, butt-forward, on his left hip, he snapped the door shut and spun the cylinder, enjoying the song it sang filled with brass. Then he picked up the reins and clucked the geldings down the left-forking trail, cautiously scanning the terrain—the pine-covered ridge to his right, the grassy hummocks and occasional boulders on his left—as he rode.

When he came to a grove of aspens, he quietly brought the geldings to a halt and set the brake. The ranch yard should be only about a hundred yards beyond the grove and around a slight curve in the trail. He'd ride no farther, but walk, approach the cabin as quietly as he could.

Hopefully, he'd be able to surprise the two robbers and anyone else in the area, and arrest them all without shooting. That had always been his goal, his challenge, to do his job without shooting, without bloodshed.

Gripping the Henry before him and releasing the leather thong over the hammer of his .44, he started cautiously through the sun-dappled shade of the trail, feeling the undeniably pleasant rush of adrenaline as he anticipated what would happen next . . . not knowing if he would live or die, kill or be killed.

9

Stillman hunkered down behind a fallen aspen at the edge of the woods and looked around. The house sat in a sunlit clearing, just beyond the big gray barn. Cloud shadows passed over the wind-buffeted grass of the yard.

Two sun-drowsing horses stood shoulder to shoulder in the corral, looking away and upwind from Stillman. The blades of the windmill squealed. The lawman was grateful for the harsh, grating noise. The squealing and the wind would cover the sound of his approach to the house.

No one appeared in the yard, but the barn doors yawned wide. A thin ribbon of smoke lifted from the house's brick chimney, torn away by the wind. There was probably someone in the barn or the house, but Stillman hoped the remaining gang members weren't spread out around the place, for he had no one to watch his back. Times like this you needed a deputy, and he was glad Leon McMannigle was on the way to Clantick. At the moment, however, he was on his own.

He crouched low at the edge of the woods and scanned the yard one more time, grateful there didn't appear to be a dog. More than one ranch raid had been foiled by a dog.

Satisfied the coast was clear, Stillman stuck his finger

through the Henry's trigger guard, lightly touching the trigger, and proceeded across the clearing toward the barn, keeping the big gray wall of the barn between him and the house. He walked slowly, watchfully, the brim of his hat tipped low against the wind.

When he came to the barn, he pressed his ear to the rough wood, listening—no sounds but the random snorts and shuffling of livestock, the trilling of pigeons in the rafters. He walked around the back and around several feed troughs and a manure pile, through waist-high pigweed, toward the house, about twenty yards from the barn. Stillman watched the two black windows intently as he approached.

He pressed his back to the house's unpainted wall and sidled up to a window, gripping the Henry and listening for voices. There were none, only the sighing of the wind against the house and the grass and the squealing windmill over the corral.

Stillman ducked beneath the window and made his way cautiously to the front of the house. At the corner he stopped and slid a careful peek at the front door. Satisfied no one had spied his approach, he stepped around the corner, his back to the wall, clutching the Henry before him.

In a half dozen steps he made the front door. Behind the screen, the inside door was open. Stillman could smell cooked food—beans and bacon—wafting through the opening.

He listened.

Finally, he turned, jerked open the screen door, and stepped inside, moving to his left and pressing his back against the wall beside the door, not offering his silhouette. The Henry was extended before him, the barrel sliding from right to left across the dusky room as Stillman's eyes adjusted.

A man sat at the plank table before Stillman, his mouth drawn wide with surprise, a plate of beans and an uncorked bottle before him. "Who the hell are you?"

"Ben Stillman, sheriff o' Clantick. I'm lookin' for your hammerheads."

"You're *what*?"

"They held up a train yesterday—my train—and two got away. But then you probably already know that, don't you?"

The man's jaw hardened and his mouth worked as he stared black hatred at Stillman. "You're the one who killed my boy."

Stillman glanced around the room. There appeared to be two more rooms behind the kitchen. "Keep your hands on the table where I can see 'em," Stillman ordered the old man as he stepped past the table, spurs singing on the planks.

Turning, he quickly inspected the room opening off to the left before swinging his gaze back to the old man, who sat stiffly in his chair, staring at Stillman with smoldering eyes.

When Stillman had checked the other room, another empty bedroom, he returned to the table and hiked a foot onto a chair, resting the Henry against the table. "Two of your boys are in the gang, I understand. Who are the rest and where are they?"

"Gone."

"Gone where?"

"None o' your fuckin' business."

"I could arrest you for harboring fugitives," Stillman warned.

The old man held out his wrists. "Arrest me."

"Are you Dillon Andrews?"

"I might be."

Stillman glanced at the doorway. "I've got three bodies outside. I'm told they belong here. If you want 'em, you can come and get 'em, or I'll toss them out on the ground, and you can bury them later."

The old man stood up suddenly, stiffly, not taking his eyes off Stillman. He didn't say anything, but his eyes grew darker by the second. Rage pulled at the corners of the old man's whiskered mouth. Stillman could smell whiskey on his breath.

"You're gonna die for killin' my boy."

Stillman ignored the threat. "Who are the others in his gang?"

"None o' your *fuckin'* business!" Andrews shouted.

"Where are they?"

"None o' your *fuckin'* business."

"Then you're under arrest for harboring fugitives and conspiring to commit a felony."

"I didn't rob no train. I was right here all the time. I ain't moved from here since my heart attack two months ago."

"But you planned it, didn't you, Pop? You're the brains, and I use that term lightly, behind this little operation. Aren't you?"

"Get the hell out of my house."

"You're comin' with me."

Andrews took two ambling steps backward. "You

can't take me to jail . . . I'll . . . I'll get sick again. I'm an old man. My heart's weak."

"You'll come with me, old and sick or not, unless you tell me where your son and the other member of your gang disappeared to."

The man's eyes rolled wildly around in their sockets as he considered what to do. Finally he took another two steps back and turned. The wall behind the range was in shadow, so Stillman couldn't tell what the old man was reaching for, but he had a bad feeling . . .

"Hold it there, Andrews!" he yelled, bringing the Henry to his chest.

The old man turned back to Stillman with a double-barreled shotgun in his hands.

"Drop it, goddamnit, or I'll shoot!" Stillman roared.

As if he hadn't heard, Dillon Andrews brought the barrel up level to his waist. He was thumbing back the rabbit-eared hammers when Stillman squeezed the Henry's trigger, the explosion echoing painfully around the room and instantly filling the air with smoke.

Andrews took the bullet in his shoulder and staggered back against the wall. Stillman considered moving around the table and grabbing the old man's two-bore, but then Dillon was bringing it to bear again.

Stillman cursed and fired another round. The slug tore through the old man's breastbone, pasting him up against the wall and jerking his head back. Andrews groaned, sighed, and slid down the wall, lowering his head to his chest. The shotgun clattered to the floor.

When Stillman had made his way around the table, Andrews was falling slowly to his side, expelling the last vestiges of air in his lungs and bowels. Out of habit,

Stillman kicked the shotgun aside and squatted on his haunches, staring at the dead man.

"Why in the hell did you have to go and pull a stupid stunt like that?" he groused.

Stillman buried Dillon Andrews and the three bodies from the wagon in a shallow grave behind the barn. If anyone wanted to give them a proper burial, the corpses wouldn't be hard to find.

Stillman was back on the trail toward Clantick by three in the afternoon. His mood was sour. His trip out here had been a fiasco. He'd had to kill another man and had learned nothing of the whereabouts of the two survivors of the train robbery.

He chided himself for not throwing the cuffs on old man Andrews up front; that way the man wouldn't have been able to go for the two-bore. Stillman had been counting on the old man telling him where the other two men had slipped off to. The old man's obvious fear of jail had indicated that's exactly what he was going to do. Stillman guessed now he hadn't realized how much the man had hated him for killing his son.

As he rode along in the heat of the afternoon, he took stock of his first few hours in Clantick. So far he'd killed four men, slapped up two more, and broken an expensive window. He wondered what the city council would have to say about all this. They were a prickly lot, and Stillman suspected he might appear a little too much like what they were afraid of—a trigger-happy gunman toting a badge.

Aside from the incident with Dillon Andrews, he didn't see much he could have done differently.

He was only about two miles from Clantick when something buzzed through the air nearby and plunked into the shoulder of one of the geldings. A distant rifle cracked as the horse jerked, bucked, and screamed, falling to its knees. Stillman grabbed his rifle and was out of the wagon in a single bound, crouching low and running for cover in a swale.

He heard the thud of two more slugs slapping the grassy sod around him, and two more rifle reports. When he'd hit the bottom of the swale on his shoulder, he scrambled to the northern lip of the depression, removed his hat, and looked around.

Grassy hummocks, golden in the west-angling light, surrounded him. Prairie dogs prattled and the wind sawed the grass.

At the same time a slug plunked into the sod about a foot from his face, he saw a powder puff tear in the wind, just above a hummock northeast of his position. A gunman lay there, at the top of the hummock, a rifle in his hands, aimed Stillman's way.

The man was jacking another shell into his rifle breech. Stillman brought the Henry up and took hasty aim and fired. From this far away, he couldn't tell where his bullet struck, but from the way the man flinched he knew his aim wasn't that far off. The man slid back off the hummock's peak, out of sight.

"Damn," Stillman grumbled.

Two quick shots rang out, and the second gelding went down, crumpling and falling against the other, dead. This made the first gelding scream all the more, and try futilely to get up, jerking the wagon around until Stillman thought it would tear it apart.

Stillman took aim and shot the gelding in the head. Both horses lay dead in their traces.

Stillman knew the man had shot the second horse so Stillman wouldn't be able to go after him. That meant the gunman had called off the kill . . . for now, anyway.

Stillman didn't want to make it easy for him. He scrambled up out of the swale and ran across the lumpy, grassy prairie to the hummock from which the man had tried to bushwack him. Reaching the hummock, he raised his rifle and rushed the peak.

The man was gone. Stillman raised his head to peer toward town. A single rider was galloping a speckle-gray horse across the prairie, dwindling in the distance toward the scattered shacks outlying Clantick. He traced a zigzagging course so Stillman couldn't get a decent bead on him. In another moment he was out of range, little more than a moving black-and-white speck on the horizon.

Casting his gaze around the hummock's rounded peak, Stillman found a handful of shell casings scattered in the grass. Scrutinizing one between his thumb and index finger, he saw it was a Springfield .45–70. Not the rarest of guns by any means, but the casing might come in handy in his identification of the gunman. He pocketed it and glanced back at the wagon, both horses dead on the trail.

"Shit."

He looked back toward the line of shacks and trees demarking town. "I'm going to get you, you son of a bitch!" he yelled, unable to contain his anger. Now he had an anonymous bushwhacker to add to his list of the day's grievous events, and to the growing catalog of problems that were his to solve on his way toward taming a town.

As he made his way toward Clantick, rifle in hand, he was seriously beginning to wonder if coming here with Fay was the biggest mistake of his life.

10

Stillman's first stop in town was the livery barn. He found Auld, the proprietor, shoeing a horse in the corral. The big, blond German with a free-ranging left eye looked sharply down at Stillman when the lawman, sitting on a hay bale to rest his hot, tired feet, had told the man what had happened to his horses.

"They're *dead*?"

"That's what I said. You'll want to send someone out for the wagon."

Auld straightened his gangly frame and dropped his shoeing hammer at his side with disgust. "I thought you came here to prevent trouble, not cause more," the German exclaimed in his low, rumbling bass.

Auld was an imposing, ham-handed, long-armed figure, with what appeared to be a knife scar above and below the injured eye. It didn't keep Stillman from losing his temper. Standing, he crossed the seven feet between him and the liveryman, giving the man a truculent grimace.

"You must have misunderstood me. I said a man on a speckle-gray shot your goddamn horses. I didn't say *I* shot them. You think I felt like taking a stroll?"

Auld took two stiff steps straight back, warily regarding the frustration and anger in Stillman's unwavering gaze and taut jaw. He defensively clutched the hammer at his thigh.

"*Comprende?*" Stillman asked after a pause.

"I hear ya," the German droned, indignant.

"You rented out any speckle-grays lately?"

"Nope."

"Know anyone around with a speckle-gray?"

Auld shook his head. "Not right off."

"Know anyone who regularly packs a forty-five–seventy Springfield?"

"Pret' near every army veteran in town."

Stillman scowled and turned away. Thoughtfully, he headed for the corral gate.

"Well, who's gonna pay for my horses?" Auld called, a note of hesitation in his voice.

"Send your bill to the city council, goddamnit," Stillman barked as he passed through the gate. "Everyone else is."

Auld pointed his hammer at him. "You . . . you got a temper. . . ."

Stillman walked up the street on his sore feet, keeping an eye out for a speckle-gray horse. He knew it was futile; the man and the horse were probably hid away somewhere that Stillman, new to the town, would never think to look. The horse would no doubt be long gone by sunrise tomorrow.

The man would still be around, however. No one but a permanent resident would have had reason to try and do away with Clantick's new lawman. Unless he was hired by someone else. . . .

It had occurred to Stillman that the shootist might have been one of the train robbers. After thinking it through, he disregarded the possibility. Not being townsmen, and therefore unable to blend into Clantick, the train robbers would have steered clear of the area. Also, the train robbers would more than likely have ambushed Stillman back in the mountains, where they could have more easily disposed of his body. There was no reason for them to wait until he was nearly to Clantick before taking a shot.

The same went for the two cowpokes he'd slapped up in Sam Wah's.

As Stillman walked along First Street toward the hotel, he remembered what Doc Evans had said about the possibility of Bernard McFadden having been the killer, or one of the killers, of Ralph Merchant. Could McFadden be the man who'd ambushed Stillman?

Why in hell would the chairman of the city council want his sheriff dead?

Befuddled, his pinstripe shirt soaked with sweat, and his dust-caked corduroy jacket thrown over his shoulder, Stillman entered the Boston and headed upstairs to his room. He knocked on the door and was happy to hear Fay's approaching footsteps. She opened the door, wrinkling her brow as she gave him a measuring stare.

"What happened to you?"

"Took a little walk," he said, kissing her, then moving into the room. He tossed his hat, coat, and rifle on the bed.

Fay closed the door and turned to him. "Looks like more than a little. Have you heard of a horse?"

"I rented two from the livery this morning. They didn't make it back."

"Oh, god. What happened?"

Stillman was unbuttoning his shirt. "Some asswipe—pardon my French—shot 'em on my way back to town."

"Oh, Ben." She helped him out of the sweat-soaked shirt, and tossed it to the floor. "Go wash," she said, motioning him to the pitcher and basin on the marble washstand, then headed for the armoire. Reaching in for a clean shirt, she turned to him with worried eyes, "Who was it? Did you see?"

Stillman doused his face with both hands and shook his head. "He was too far away. Tried to drygulch me, the son of a bitch."

"You haven't been in town long enough to make any enemies . . . have you?"

He decided not to tell her about the two brutes in Sam Wah's, or about Dillon Andrews. She'd no doubt find out soon enough. "Who the hell knows, in a place like this?"

"What do you mean?"

He told her about Doc Evans's suspicion that Bernard McFadden had killed Ralph Merchant.

"Why?"

"He doesn't know."

"That sounds a little farfetched to me. I met his wife this afternoon—she invited me to tea. She seems like a very nice person."

Stillman ran a towel down his face and under his arms. "Sounds a little unlikely to me, too," he said, thoughtfully. "I think it's going to take me a while to get a handle on this here little berg. I get the feeling very little is as it seems."

He looked up to see her watching him, concern creasing the corners of her eyes.

"I sure am happy to see you," he said, tossing the towel on a bedpost, moving toward her and taking her in his arms. He hugged her tightly.

"Ben . . . maybe we should leave."

He held her away from him and gazed into her face. "What do you mean—run?"

Fay shrugged.

"Honey, we've been over this. We both read Jody's letters. We knew it wasn't going to be any strip-and-go-naked picnic up here."

Fay looked down, deeply troubled. "I know, but . . . someone tried to kill you today."

"And I'm gonna find the bastard!"

"What if he finds you first?"

"I'll be watching for him."

"Oh, Ben."

"Fay, don't do this. We talked about this."

"I know . . . I'm just . . . so afraid of losing you."

He took her shoulders in his hands and tipped his head to look into her downcast eyes. "Please don't worry, Fay."

She lifted her chin to meet his gaze, forced a smile. He was right. They'd talked about this. She had to be strong. This was the life they'd chosen. "Just don't get yourself killed, Mr. Stillman, or I'm going to be very upset." She turned her head to kiss his hand. "I love you."

"I love you, Fay."

Her mood lightening, she smiled. "Are you taking me to dinner?"

"Later. I have to meet Leon." He took the clean shirt she was holding and slipped it on.

"I can't wait to see him again."

Stillman chuckled as he buttoned the shirt. "I can't wait for that myself. I think he'll make a damn good deputy, and a hell of a nice guy to have around. From the look of things, Clantick could use a nice guy."

"You can say that again," Fay said. "Mrs. McFadden told me someone beat up one of the flophouse girls last week. She died the day we came in on the train."

"Oh, Jesus," Stillman said with a pained expression. "Anyone know who did it?"

"A drunk cowboy, they think. No one knows for sure." Fay turned, walked to one of the room's two windows, and pulled up the shade. "The funeral is going on right now."

Knotting his string tie, Stillman walked over to the window and stopped beside his wife. He followed her gaze over the darkening rooftops of the business district.

Westward, a cemetery perched on a flat butte, the haphazardly arranged stones silhouetted against the west-falling sun. Also silhouetted were ten or twelve women carrying flowers. Another woman stood separate from the others, facing the group with her head inclined over an open book in her hands.

"As if their lives aren't tough enough," Stillman growled.

"It's happened before," Fay said. "Several of the girls have been beaten to death in the past year."

Stillman looked at her. "By the same guy?"

Fay shrugged. "I guess they don't know."

"I guess I'd better find out," Stillman said, turning his gaze back to the cemetery, where the mourners were tossing their flowers in a hole.

After a moment, he turned, kissed his wife on the

cheek, and retrieved his hat from the bed. He headed for the door. "I'll be back in a bit."

Fay turned to him. "Ben," she called as he opened the door. "You be careful!"

Stillman smiled and touched his hat. "I wouldn't have it any other way, Mrs. Stillman."

He closed the door and was gone.

Fay stared at the door and listened to his footsteps in the hall and on the stairs, frowning. Then she turned to watch the mourners on the butte.

Stillman entered the station house as the six-ten chugged onto the siding. The station agent, a large balding man in rolled sleeves, blue wool vest, and uniform hat, stood just beyond the doors, the smoke from his stogey mixing with the steam and cinder smoke expunged by the sighing steel locomotive. The soot-covered fireman in the tender car smiled and waved when he saw Stillman, unable to conceal his relief at making Clantick just in time for supper and a tall pilsner.

The conductor stepped down from the train and positioned a step stool for the disembarking passengers. Two children in ill-fitting homespuns did not wait for the step, however. They jumped down off the vestibule, ignoring the conductor's chastising remarks, and went running down the platform.

"Come find me, Harry!" the little girl yelled to her brother, long blond hair fanning out behind her, scuffed leather shoes tapping on the cobblestone platform.

"Melissa!" a woman yelled from an open window. "You *wait!*"

Had he ever been that age? Stillman wondered, staring after the retreating girl and boy.

"Dependin' I guess on what your lovely wife has to say about it, you could have a whole passel o' those," a deep male voice announced in his ear.

Turning, Stillman saw the grinning black face of Leon McMannigle. "Not at my age," the lawman said. He grinned and hugged his old friend, then held him at arm's length, smiling into his face. "You're lookin' fit as a year-old rooster!"

"But not half as much like struttin'. You'd think with 'progress' and all they could make a train seat that didn't cripple a man."

"We'll get a drink in you, and you'll heal up in no time."

"Now, there's the answer I was lookin' for!" Leon's eyes slitted as he smiled, chuckling deep in his chest.

He wore a floppy black hat and a light wool coat over a black cowhide vest and white shirt with red pinstripes and a poet's collar. He stood an inch or so shorter than Stillman, but was thick-necked, broad-shouldered, and muscular. He looked like a boxer, which he had been, albeit an amateur, when he'd ridden in the Ninth Cavalry down in Arizona, chasing Apaches. As he smiled, his square teeth shone whitely against the big, finely chiseled mahogany face and large, round, night-black eyes glinting with warmth and friendliness.

"Good to see ya again, Ben."

"Thanks for coming."

"Hey, when I got your letter, I knew there was no other way. When the great Ben Stillman asks you for help, you come a-runnin'."

"I hope I didn't pull you away from something too important."

"Nah, I was just tendin' bar down in Julesburg, waitin' for the next-best-thing to come along. I'm glad you thought of me, but you know I never worn no badge before." He held his hands up, palms out. "I'll tell ya that, right off."

"I know that," Stillman nodded. "But you saved my ass more than a few times up here two years ago, and I know your service record. I can't think of anyone who'd better fit the job description, or who I'd trust more with my backside." Stillman turned to gesture at the luggage car. "Any bags?"

"Just this here," Leon said, lifting his canvas war bag.

"Traveling light," Stillman said.

"Well, not by choice." The black man winced. "I lost pret' near everything in a card game. Damn near had to give the man my shirt! Turns out he was cheatin'—one o' these riverboat gamblers, you know—but I didn't find that out till the next day. By that time he was way on down the Miss'ippi."

"Damn the luck," Stillman allowed. "Come on, I'll give you a little tour of the town—if you're not too tired."

"Hell, I been sittin' for two days."

The player pianos were already clattering their tinny renditions of "Yellow Rose of Texas" and "Sweet Betsy from Pike," and most of the hitching racks before the saloons were filled with tail-swishing ranch mounts as Stillman led his new deputy down the boardwalks.

"Wet your whistle?" Stillman asked, stopping outside the Goliad saloon.

"Hell, I could drown it," McMannigle chuffed, turning and pushing through the batwings.

He'd no sooner stepped into the big, smoky room filled with cowboys and working girls than the piano clattered to a slow stop as the man playing it turned to see what had silenced the crowd. Nearly everyone in the room had turned to regard Stillman and McMannigle with incredulous, hostile eyes.

"Uh-uh, not in here," the bartender said, a big, round-faced man with small, dumb eyes and a black beard. "They'll serve a nigger across the street. I won't serve ya in here. No one will this side o' First."

"Well, I'm sorry to hear that," Leon said, obviously accustomed to such treatment. He turned to Stillman and said with mocking gravity, "Ben, we have to go across the street."

Stillman brushed past him to the bar. "My feet are too sore to walk across the street. I'll have my beer here and so will you." Stillman dropped a coin on the bar. "Two tall ones. I'm changing the rules. This is my deputy, and he'll drink wherever he damn well pleases." He met the barman's insolent stare and drew his coat back to reveal the star on his chest.

"You're the new sheriff? You're Stillman?"

"That's right."

"Well, shit."

"And you're . . ."

"Ralph Avery. I'm half owner o' this place."

"Who owns the other half?"

Avery shrugged and said smugly, "Can't tell you that. Silent partner."

"Well, tell your silent partner the rules have

changed—as far as my deputy's concerned, anyway. We'll work at changing the rest of it later."

"He ain't gonna like it."

"I don't care if he likes it," Stillman said.

The barman looked around as if for help. A man in a black hat funneled low over his eyes scraped his chair back and stood. Another, shorter man with a dusty cream hat and drooping mustaches brusquely shoved the pleasure girl off his knee, and gained his feet, as well. Both men sauntered over to Stillman and McMannigle.

The tall man smiled with his lips but the cold eyes made it a lie. "Evenin', Sheriff," the man said. He spat tobacco juice on the floor near Leon's boot.

Stillman did not reply. He watched both men coolly, knowing he had to keep an eye on the rest of the room, as well. You never knew when some anonymous drunk hammerhead would pull an iron.

"So you're ol' Stillman, eh?" the shorter man in the cream hat said, a mocking smile twisting his lips.

"And this is Leon McMannigle, my deputy," Stillman announced to the entire room. The place was so silent you could practically hear the dust sifting from the rafters.

All eyes were on Stillman and McMannigle.

"Heard you were washed up," the tall man said, staring at Stillman.

"Well, that's a step up for me. Most think I'm dead."

"That might just be arranged, after what you did to ol' Claude and Jory over at Sam Wah's this mornin'. Nobody slaps around Mr. Billingsley's men, breaks a guy's nose, and gets away with it. Those are just the rules around here, and I think the sooner you learn 'em, why . . . the better off you'll be."

"Is that right?" Stillman said. He hooked his thumbs in the riveted pockets of his jeans and inclined his head, giving the tall cowboy a mock serious eye. "While we're on the subject, any more rules I should know about?"

"Well, for one, no niggers are allowed in the Goliad—even niggers some washed-up ol' lawman dredged up from the bottom o' the watermelon barrel and gave a badge 'cause no one else'd be stupid enough to work for him."

Leon scratched his chin and glanced at Stillman. "I'm not sure, but I think one of us was just insulted, Ben."

Stillman smiled at the cowboy. "Any more?"

The cowboy glanced back at the onlooking crowd, smiled smugly, and turned back to Stillman as he cocked his arm to throw a punch. Stillman ducked, and the cowboy's fist thrashed air. With a sharp right, Stillman jabbed the man in the belly so hard he could feel his spine, and heard several ribs crack. The man gave an explosive grunt, which echoed around the room, and crumpled to his knees with a thump, sending up sawdust from the floor.

The other cowboy cursed and stepped toward Stillman, but before he could cross the three-foot gap between them, Leon brought up his right foot and smashed it down hard on the man's left ankle, as though he were killing a particularly large rodent. The sound was like a branch breaking over a man's knee. The cowboy screamed and staggered back and sideways, bringing down a table and scattering several cowboys and a pleasure girl as he fell. He clutched his awkwardly hanging ankle, cursing and yelling, *"That nigger broke my foot!"*

Most of the room was on its feet. A drover with long-ish salt-and-pepper hair and a pale, long face bolted out from the crowd, getting a clear path for a bullet, and drew his revolver. He fired, smoke and flames geysering from the gun.

The bullet whistled past Stillman's ear and broke a bottle on the back bar. Stillman's .44 was in his hand in a split second. He automatically thumbed back the hammer, squeezed the trigger, and plugged the man through the throat. The man clutched his neck, turned, ran to the back of the room, bounced off the wall, and hit the floor shaking as he died.

Stillman brought his gun to bear on the rest of the crowd. Glancing to his side, he saw McMannigle reliev-ing the barman of a two-bore shotgun and holding his own Colt at the man's head. "Never did like the notion of gettin' backshot by a farm gun," he said to the man, who glared at him.

Stillman said to the crowd. "Anyone else got any more rules they want to lay down?"

The cowboys and pleasure girls were murmuring un-der the lamps set to swinging from the rafters by all the commotion.

"Good. Then I'll tell you mine. As of this evening, my good deputy here will go anywhere he damn well pleases in this town, and you'll show him the same re-spect you would to anyone else wearing the official badge of sheriff of Hill County. Also, you'll all behave as nice as choirboys while you're visiting our fair city, and just to help you along the path of righteousness you'll wear no guns on your persons after eight o'clock in the evening. Anyone caught with so much as a .22 derringer in their boot after said hour will find themselves in the hothouse."

The murmurs had risen to such a fervor that Stillman's last sentence had been drowned out by the din. He looked at McMannigle, shook his head, and fired a bullet into the floor.

Silence. All eyes turned to him again.

He repeated his last sentence and asked if anyone needed elaboration or clarification. They all stared at him with hushed truculence. He knew they all wanted to hang him and Leon from the nearest tree and would have if they'd had the chance.

"In light of what has happened here tonight, I'm afraid I'm going to have to move up the time for disarmament to now. Everyone form an orderly line and drop your sidearms and any other weapon on your person in the corner up there by the window."

A roar went up like a cannon. Stillman fired another round into the floor.

"Those are the rules here and everywhere else in town. Get a move on. I want to see a nice pile of weapons. Move!"

The cowboys grudgingly formed a line as they moved to the front corner of the room, unhitching their gunbelts and dropping them by the window. As the line progressed, Stillman and McMannigle covering the room with their revolvers, Stillman said, "I reserve the right to spot check every saloon in town. Anyone I catch with a gun will get three days and a twenty-dollar fine."

Several cowboys sitting at the back of the room looked at one another. They sighed, got reluctantly to their feet, and joined the procession. A few others headed for the door.

"Those are the rules for the whole town," Stillman reminded them. He turned to Leon. "I hope you're not too tired to start right away. I'll swear you in later."

Leon chuckled, watching the procession with humorous eyes. "Hell, I wouldn't miss this for the world." He thought of something and his brow furrowed. "How are we going to keep an eye on all these saloons?"

"We'll just have to spot check them," Stillman said. "Eventually these men will realize they have to toe up or lose their month's wages and spend three days in the icebox. The bartenders will help. We'll shut them down if they're not enforcing the rule."

"Good idea," Leon said. He shook his head and whistled. "But I'll tell ya one thing . . . I haven't felt this unpopular since they passed the 'Mancipation Proclamation."

When the room was disarmed and all the cowboys and pleasure girls had retaken their seats—the ones who'd stayed—Stillman and McMannigle got their beers from the disgruntled bartender and took seats with their backs to the wall. The injured men were helped out of the saloon. Two cowboys had taken the dead man up to the coroner and returned to finish their drinks. Stillman filled Leon in on what had happened in the twenty-four hours since he and Fay had arrived.

When he'd finished with the story of the man who'd tried to bushwack him, Leon shook his head and whistled for the twelfth time in the last half hour.

"So watch your back is what I'm sayin'," Stillman said, lifting the schooner to his lips for another sip of the ale. "I don't know if it was just me the rifleman was after or the badge. If it was the badge, he'll be after you, too."

Licking foam from his mustache, Stillman smiled at the expression on his new deputy's face. "So what do you think of the job so far?"

Leon stared at him uncertainly, his brown eyes wide with disbelief. "Sheee-it . . ."

Unobserved by Stillman, one of the men in the saloon was glaring at him from across the room, a particularly malevolent gleam in his eyes. He'd pulled his hat down low to hide his face, so that Stillman couldn't recognize him.

The man elbowed his partner, E. L. "Scratch" Lawson. "That's him, sure enough."

"That's who?"

"The sheriff . . . Stillman. That's the man on the train who shot Howie and the others."

"You sure?"

"I'd recognize him, that hat and that mustache, anywheres."

Scratch eyed Stillman cautiously, keeping his head turned a little askance. "Well . . . shit, we can't . . . we can't . . . Hell, he's bigger than . . . Good with a gun, too."

"Tell that to Pa," Bob Andrews growled at his cousin.

Scratch sighed. "Oh, boy. What are we gonna do?"

"Wait," Bob said, still staring at the lawman across the room. "Just wait . . . for the right moment."

"Then . . ."

Bob turned to Scratch with a sour grin etched on his lips. "We get 'im."

11

The next morning, Jody Harmon was awakened with a shotgun blast that rattled the windows of the small, three-bedroom cabin he and Crystal had built on the same spot as his father and mother had built theirs nearly twenty years ago.

He bolted upright in bed, heart pounding, and looked around the misty, dawn-lit room slowly swimming into focus. He flung the covers aside and was about to reach for his holstered Remington on the chair beside the bed when he realized Crystal was not in the room.

He sat on the edge of the bed with one foot dangling to the floor and pondered the situation.

Any man married to any ordinary woman would have felt alarmed, hearing a shotgun blast at such an hour and then finding his wife gone. But Jody Harmon was married to no ordinary woman. Rather than feel concerned for Crystal's safety, he found himself concerned for the safety of the creature, human or otherwise, that may have wandered into the yard while Jody's bride was out using the privy.

Through the open window he heard footsteps. The front door squeaked open and banged shut.

"Crystal?"

Boots clomped up the stairs, growing in volume as

they neared the bedroom, the heels scuffing the rough planks.

Crystal appeared in the open door, shotgun in hand. She was wearing cowboy boots with undershot heels, a battered felt cowboy hat banded with silver conchos, and a pair of Jody's red long johns so old and threadbare they clung sheerly to the young woman's sensual curves. Unbuttoned as they were to the waist, they hid very little of her firm, white breasts.

"Found a skunk in the privy."

Jody stared at her, dumbfounded by the enticing figure the girl could trace without even trying. "Huh?"

She walked into the room, removed the cowboy hat, and shook out her long blond hair. "Found a skunk in the privy," she repeated, tossing her hat on a peg behind the door.

She sat on the bed, hiked a foot on her knee, and started removing the boot. "Sorry 'bout all the noise, but I've been after that skunk for a week now. He could stink the whole yard up worse than the privy itself!" She tossed the boot on the floor and went to work on the other. "Well . . . I outskunked him!" she said, heaving the other boot off, then tossing it down with the other.

She turned to Jody apologetically. "I hope you can go back to sleep."

"I don't think so."

"Huh?"

He was leaning forward to kiss her half-bare shoulder. He slid his hand inside her long johns and cupped a breast.

"Hey," she breathed. "What do you think you're do-ing?"

"You started it."

"I didn't start nothin'. I was just out blastin' a skunk out of the privy."

"In my long johns."

"So?"

"Seein' you in those long johns, holding a shotgun, just plum pesters me to death. Get out of 'em."

He fondled her nipple and kissed her mouth. She opened her lips and pressed her tongue against his. "You're supposed to be sleepin'. You got work today."

"Get out of those long johns."

She giggled. "Okay."

She bounced to her feet, peeled the long johns down her arms and legs, kicked her feet free, and climbed back into bed. She straddled Jody, who reached up to caress her breasts, and bent her head so that her long, straight hair brushed his chest.

They made love tenderly, adeptly, with none of the awkwardness of their first few months together. They knew each other now, could play each other like familiar instruments.

They sighed and groaned, rocking together. At length they turned over, switching positions, the springs of the old bed chirping softly at first, then with building rancor, the scarred headboard finally pounding the log wall with solid, measured beats before suddenly growing still.

The bed gave a final shudder. Jody rolled onto his back and Crystal rested her head on his chest, swallowing, breathing heavily, her skin slick with sweat. They dozed that way, wrapped in each other's arms, for a half hour.

Then Crystal stirred, lifted her lips to Jody's, kissed

him, slipped out of bed, and dressed leisurely . . . hoping against hope she was pregnant at last.

It was time. They weren't kids anymore. . . .

She washed at the outside well, toweled dry, then returned to the cabin to light the range for breakfast. She heard Jody moving around upstairs, dressing. In a few minutes she had the eggs and bacon frying in a cast-iron skillet, and coffee perking in the big, black percolator. Jody appeared, tucking his shirt into his pants. He came up behind her at the range, encircled her in his arms, and nuzzled her neck.

She laughed. "That tickles."

"Think we have a bun in the oven?"

"I don't know," she cooed with a grin, turning from the stove with the pan of scrambled eggs in her hand. "I guess we'll know before long." Her smile belied her worry. They'd been trying for several months now, and nothing had happened.

"Maybe we can give it another shot after lunch . . . just in case," Jody said, giving his wife a wink and sitting down to table.

"Jody Harmon, you're gonna wear it out!"

Jody laughed and dug into his breakfast. When he finished, he kissed Crystal, and headed outside. Crystal followed him out when she'd finished washing the dishes and straightening up the kitchen, swabbing down the table and plank countertops.

She was saddling a skewbald gelding named Earl when Jody pulled out of the barn on a buckboard wagon drawn by a two-horse team. The back of the wagon was stacked with picks, shovels, saws, a shotgun, a fence stretcher, and a dozen blocks of salt. He was heading into the back country to scout the line, checking on calves, cleaning out creeks that beavers might have dammed, and dropping salt blocks.

He pulled up near his wife. "Where you headin'?" he asked.

Crystal turned to him, hesitating. Her plans for the day had been long in the scheming, and she was not sure she wanted to share them with Jody. They were as close as a husband and wife could be, but what she felt compelled to do today she had to do in secret. She wasn't sure how Jody would feel about it, and, what's more, she wasn't sure how she felt about it herself.

The whole thing made her feel guilty and withdrawn.

She turned to him and fashioned a smile. "I'm gonna ride over and see how Mrs. Nielsgaard is doing with her baby, and give ol' Nip a long-needed workout along the way."

"Are you sure that's all you're gonna do?"

Crystal narrowed her eyes at her husband. "What do you mean?" she said, defensively.

Jody shrugged, taken aback by her reply. "I figured maybe you were gonna get a few pointers."

"Pointers?"

"Well, yeah. Kirstie Nielsgaard has had seven babies now, hasn't she?"

"Oh," Crystal said, relieved. "Pointers . . . yes. You're right. A woman with seven babies is bound to teach me something about raising a family."

Jody cocked his head. "Crystal, are you all right?"

"What do you mean?"

"You're actin' strange all of a sudden."

"I'm fine. I guess it's just this heat . . . so early in the day. You know how I hate it hot, and it's gonna get darn hot today."

"Well, stop at the creek and have you a swim," Jody said. Then he smiled. "If you're in my neck of the woods, maybe I'll join you."

"I don't think you're talking about swimming, Jody Harmon," Crystal admonished, tightening her saddle's latigo and giving her husband a false sneer, getting a little of her composure back.

"No, I'm not!" Jody whooped. He tossed his reins, and the harnessed geldings moved out toward the Texas gate.

"Jody," Crystal called to his back, "I love you!"

"I love you, too!" Jody shouted back.

In a moment he was gone, the dust settling in the warm morning sun behind him, and Crystal was alone again with her troubled thoughts. Frowning, she climbed into the saddle, clucked to Nip, and headed out through the Texas gate, hanging a sharp right and crossing the dew-dappled pasture behind the barn.

When she came to the grave along the creek, she halted the horse beneath the cottonwoods. This was where Mr. Harmon, Jody's father, used to sit summer evenings after chores, and dangle a worm into the creek's wide, deep pool. That's why Jody had buried him here. It had been his favorite place, where he and Jody's mother, a Cree woman named Tah-kwa-i-mi-nah-nah, had settled the year before Jody was born.

Casting her dark gaze at the stone marker, Crystal saw that the grass around the rock-mounded grave had been trampled flat by Jody, who came here nearly every day to offer a silent prayer. Crystal came here, too, whenever she could bring herself. The grave was a haunting reminder of her own father's violence, for it had been him, Warren Johnson, who had killed Bill Harmon.

When she had learned that impossible, horrible fact, she had wanted to die. It had been Jody's love that had pulled her back from the edge. Her father's ghastly crime could have driven a wedge between them and withered their love. In the end, however, it became the rage and sadness that bound them.

"I'm sorry, Mr. Harmon," she said quietly now, as she always did, and reined the horse across the creek and up the gently sloping ridge, through the thickets of juneberry and wild rose, hawthorn spikes scratching her jeans.

She crossed the ridge, descended the other side, and followed the draw to Wild Raspberry Hollow. When she came to a slope covered with bright wildflowers, she stopped, tied Nip to a branch, and picked a handful of shooting star and balsam root, adding some white campion and a few stems of red four o'clock for contrast.

Gently clutching the bouquet in her gloved hand, she climbed back onto the gelding and spurred him into a walk, then a trot. Five minutes later, coming out of a shady aspen hollow, she turned onto an old wagon trail, nearly overgrown for lack of use. The road curved over the saddle between Big John Butte and Bear Ridge, and plunged into Holbrook Valley. Near a rocky dike halfway down the mountain, she halted her horse and cast her gaze to the valley floor.

The small ranch headquarters her father had built and where Crystal had been raised nestled in the treeless hollow. The log house, barn, and corrals were sinking into ruin. Pigweed and wild rye nearly hid the wooden tank beneath the windmill, and several shakes had blown off the cabin's roof. Rain had found the vacancy and chewed gaping holes through the pine.

All that stirred and showed any sign of life were the weeds, buffeted by the wind, and the swallows wheeling in and out of the open barn doors. Behind the cabin, the outhouse door squeaked. It was an eerie, lonely sound here, where a family had once lived and been scattered to the four winds by one man's lonely, drunken rage.

Tears welled in Crystal's eyes as she studied her childhood home. They were not tears of nostalgia, for she missed nothing about the place, where her father drank and raged, cowing his wife and children into phantoms of their true selves. What she missed was the rest of her family—her mother, Bess, and her brothers and sisters, most of whom had left the area as soon as they'd turned sixteen. Jason, the youngest, had left when he was only fourteen, having landed a job putting up tents for a traveling carnival show.

Only Crystal's sister, Marie, remained in the Two Bears, on a ranch with her husband, Ivan, who drank and whored and beat Marie senseless for such mishaps as overcooking his eggs. Their mother had gone to live in Idaho with a railroad man she'd met after leaving Crystal's father and while cleaning Great Northern passenger cars in Clantick. Crystal received letters from her once or twice a year—brief, sketchy narratives about her life with Roy, who, it sounded, was little better than Crystal's father had been.

Crystal never heard from the others in her family. She only hoped that they, unlike Marie and their mother, had somehow survived and overcome the damage of Warren Johnson's dark legacy.

Crystal spurred her horse down the hill. She rode out into the field that rose eastward beyond the house, toward a knob. There was a wood marker on the knob, and as Crystal approached, she slid down from her saddle and dropped Earl's reins. She'd trained him not to wander.

Crickets chirped, grasshoppers arced over the waving weeds, and brush wrens flitted here and there, chortling.

Crystal climbed the knob, holding the flowers in her fist. She had not seen the marker, for she had never visited the grave. Two years ago, three months after Ben Stillman had left Clantick with Fay, Jody had found her father dead in the cabin. Whether his body had given out from the alcohol or he'd frozen to death was hard to say. He hadn't been arrested for killing Jody's father, because Ben, Jody, and Crystal had decided no incarceration could have been worse than the one he was living in his decrepit body and damaged mind. It was obvious from his pumpkin-sized liver that he was close to the end.

When Jody discovered his body, he went to town and got the sheriff. They stored the body in the barn. When the ground thawed in the spring, Jody rode over alone, without Crystal, and buried it here on the knob. Crystal had wanted the old man to rot in the cabin, but Jody thought that every person, no matter how they had lived or what they had done, should at least be buried.

Now Crystal walked up to the simple wooden cross Jody had made from two green pine branches and rawhide. She felt a constriction in her chest and a heaviness in her stomach. Her upper lip quivered. A tear dribbled down her cheek. She knelt and covered her mouth with her hand to quell a sob.

Why had she suddenly felt the overwhelming need to visit the grave? He was the most evil man Crystal had ever known, and he'd done the worst thing a man could do.

Still . . . he'd been her father . . .

She didn't know what made her feel worse—knowing what he had done, or knowing she was his daughter and that there was nothing she could do to change that horrible fact.

She lay her hand on one of the rocks over the grave. She brought up her other hand and set the flowers among the stones, nestling them in a hollow, away from the wind. She looked around, feeling somehow guilty and illicit for what she did, putting flowers on such a man's grave. He had killed Bill Harmon, after all. Her husband's father. But deep inside she felt a nagging, undeniable need to forgive him for that, and to begin to try to make peace with the man.

She stood up slowly and regarded the flowers in the rocks. "There you go," she said. "I want you to know that I hate you, but I'm trying to forgive you. I'm trying to forgive myself for being part of you. Every year on this day, your birthday, I'll come out here and put flowers on your grave. But that's all I'll do. I won't think of you on any day but this. I won't let you haunt me in death like you did in life. I have to accept what you did and let you go, and you have to let me go."

Suddenly her face crumpled and tears rushed over her cheeks. "Oh, shit!" she cried, cocking one hip and folding her arms angrily across her chest. "Why?" she cried, her voice small with inconsolable pain. "Why . . . ?"

Finally, the tears abated. Crystal wiped her cheeks with her hands. She turned and started down the knob, toward her horse idly cropping grass.

She stopped and turned back to regard the wooden cross. "Good-bye," she said.

Inexplicably feeling lighter, feeling better, she turned again and walked away. And she didn't look back.

12

Leon McMannigle dipped his razor in the basin of cold water. Cocking his head in the mirror over the wash-stand, he scraped the blade along his jaw, the coarse black hair rolling up into the white shave cream like dirt plowed up with snow.

After three or four more strokes, he paused, catching the wary look in his dark eye. He stared back at it, scru-tinizing it, as though the face were not his own.

"Was I crazy, coming here?" he asked himself aloud.

A female voice mumbled something behind him. He turned to the girl on the bed. A lovely brunette named Darla, she lay facedown with a sheet twisted just below her plump, naked buttocks. It had been a hot night, and here on the second story of the no-name place with the sign over the street announcing rooms by the hour, nary a breeze had discovered the open windows until nearly four o'clock in the morning.

"Sorry, Precious," Leon cooed to the girl, holding the razor in one hand, the shaving mug in the other. "I was just talkin' to myself. You go on sleepin'."

The girl mumbled something unintelligible and sighed.

Leon smiled and turned back to the mirror. The smile faded as his thoughts resumed their course.

He touched a finger to the bright purple knot on his

swollen lip—the result of a punch delivered by a drunk in Howell's saloon, where Leon and Stillman had ended up last night. They'd been summoned by several shots delivered by a cowboy trying to shoot his partner for cheating at cards. The targeted man had escaped injury by crawling under tables. It had helped that his pistol-wielding partner was too drunk to shoot straight, but he'd nearly gunned down several innocent bystanders in his attempt to kill his friend.

Stillman and McMannigle were able to sneak up behind the man, subdue him, and take his gun away. While Stillman stayed in Howell's saloon to announce the new rules to the crowd, Leon led the drunk gunman over to the jailhouse. On the way, the man had slipped his right hand out of Leon's grasp, and laid his fist against Leon's lower lip before the deputy was able to shove the man down on the boardwalk and knock the fight out of him with a punch.

Leon had lived near here when he'd met Stillman two years ago. He'd run a roadhouse down near the Missouri River breaks, serving stew and beer to transient cow-pokes and freighters driving teams back and forth between the river and a handful of little towns in north-central Montana. It had been a good life, and he'd shared it, for a while, with a half-breed Indian girl he'd called Mary Beth. She'd been "touched," and had never told him her real name, if she even had one. She was killed, like so many, in the trouble Donovan Hobbs had instigated when he'd started "weeding out" the small ranchers in the Two Bears.

In a way, this was familiar territory to Leon, but it had changed more than a little since he'd been away.

When Stillman had cabled him in Julesburg, asking him to join him in Clantick as deputy sheriff, Leon had hesitated nary thirty seconds before dictating an affirmative reply. In spite of Stillman's warning, coming second-hand from Jody Harmon, it was hard to imagine the little frontier town on the Milk River as having grown into another Dodge City or Abilene. Hell, when Leon had been there, it had been home to maybe three hundred people, half of them blanket Indians and transient drovers!

He'd always liked the big, open country around the Two Bears—before the Hobbs trouble, that is—and he thought he'd like to return to it and settle down. The deputy sheriff's job wouldn't be all that different from the work he'd done soldiering with the Ninth Cavalry down in Arizona. Probably a lot less strenuous. There was no way, unless the old Apache war chief Nana had decided to head north, it could be even half as dangerous.

Or could it? he asked himself now, running his tongue over the swollen lip.

It wasn't just his damaged lip that unsettled him. It was everything Stillman had told him as they'd walked from saloon to saloon last night. The train robbery, the troublemakers in Sam Wah's café, old man Andrews, the fellow on the speckle-gray who'd tried to drygulch Ben, and the dead whore—one of many in the past year.

That was a mess of trouble for Stillman to have met within less than twenty-four hours. . . .

At thirty, Leon was no spring chicken. He'd had an uncomplicated life in Julesburg, serving up liquor to gamblers and pleasure girls. Since the saloon had not belonged to him, he could leave it every night and not think about it until his next shift. In his off hours he'd ridden out in the country and fished and drank beer with the old black men who gathered nightly in a sandwich shop down by the river.

Now he suddenly felt as though he'd been shanghaied to serve on some pirate ship populated by thugs. Only the captain was a man he respected and admired, and felt proud and flattered to serve. That was the problem. He liked Stillman too much to turn tail and run, no matter how complicated and dangerous his life had suddenly become.

Leon toweled his face dry and turned to the brunette on the bed. And you had to admit . . . the job's fringe benefits were not bad. Especially when most of these northern girls had never seen a black man before, and were . . . well . . . curious.

"I'll see you later, sugar," he whispered in the girl's ear, bending over the bed. He'd buckled on his gunbelt and grabbed his black hat, ready to go.

The girl turned to him, mussed hair in her squinting eyes, smacking her lips. She wrapped her arms around his neck and snuggled against him. "Lee-on, why are you up so *early*?"

McMannigle sighed, fingered the deputy sheriff's star on his shirt, and faked a wince. "Sugar . . . a man's work is never done."

"Will you come back and see me again soon?"

"How's tonight sound?"

"I'll be here, Leon." Eyes closed, the girl smiled, lay her head on the pillow, and drifted back to sleep.

Leon stood, took a parting look at the girl's sumptuous physique, shook his head, whistled softly, then headed for the door. "I don't know what's gonna kill me first," he said, latching the door softly behind him. "This town full of badasses or this town full of pleasure girls."

He'd taken two steps down the dim hall when he heard voices raised in anger—a woman's and a man's. Just beneath the heated conversation could be heard the sound of a woman, or a girl, crying.

It was not unheard of for a man and woman to argue in a brothel. But there was something in these two voices, and in the girl's crying, that caused Leon to pause outside their door. The man's speech was more cultivated than you usually heard in such a place. Both he and the woman were making an effort, however feeble, to keep their voices low. They were obviously arguing about something they didn't want others to know about.

". . . and I paid for her, by god!" the man roared.

The sound of angry footsteps rose, and the door opened before Leon could decide what to do. Suddenly a man in a well-tailored suit stood before him, staring, his face flushed with anger. Leon stared back, warm with embarrassment. He didn't like eavesdropping, but this might have been a situation for the law.

"And just what in the hell do you think you're doing?" the man rasped, jaws clenched.

Leon raised his hands placatingly, but before he could speak the man's eyes drifted to the deputy's star pinned to McMannigle's vest. He raised his eyes again to Leon's, appearing suddenly alarmed. Without another word, he turned on his heel, donned his slouch hat, and walked down the hall, descending the stairs at the other end.

Leon leaned toward the door, listening. After a moment he tapped on it with the backs of his knuckles. "Everything all right?" he called softly.

The door opened. The lady Leon recognized as the one who ran the place opened the door. Her name, he'd learned, was Mrs. Lee. She was a slender, hard-looking woman with her hair pulled back in a taut bun, stretching the skin over her forehead so that she appeared slightly bug-eyed. She could have been any honyonker's wife.

"Nothin's happenin' here that I can't take care of, Deputy," she said tightly. Then she closed the door. Shortly, the girl stopped crying.

"Are you sure?" Leon called.

When he got no reply, he continued down the hall and descended the stairs, shaking his head.

Leon had breakfast over at Sam Wah's, behind the rough pine boards Wah had nailed over the window frame. The glass the café owner had ordered from the mercantile would not arrive for several weeks.

The plywood blocked the morning sun and compelled Wah to light the lanterns, but the proprietor didn't seem all that disturbed. He whistled while he hustled between the kitchen and the counter, where Leon dipped his toast in his easy-over eggs, then skipped around the counter to refill the coffee cups of the handful of other diners scattered about the room. It was a chaste crowd of suited men, and women in conservative dresses. There were only three cowboys in the place—all on their best behavior.

When Leon had first entered, removing his hat, Sam had seen the star on his chest. He'd grinned broadly, hustled over, and pumped Leon's hand. "You new law, too? Good, good. That Steel-man, he kick ass good!"

Leon chuckled. "That he does, Mr. Wah. That he does . . ."

After breakfast, Leon made his morning rounds, introducing himself to the proprietors out cleaning their front windows or sweeping dust and cigar butts off their boardwalks. Several shook his hand reluctantly, distrustful of his color, but most were openly friendly. He knew that most of the people up here, excepting those from the South, had never seen a black man before. It would take some time, people being people, for them to get comfortable with his presence. It would probably take them a little longer to work their minds around a black man wearing a badge, just as it had taken time for the white army to get used to negroes wearing uniforms.

Most would come around, he knew. As for the others, well . . . he'd just have to ignore them as long as they ignored him—and didn't break the law. That's just the way it was, and you could piss and moan all you wanted, but nothing changed as slowly as attitudes.

Around eleven o'clock it was getting hot enough that he started looking for some shade in which to rest his legs a spell. He came to the Goliad saloon and heard a commotion inside. It sounded like two men arguing. He turned through the batwings and stood there, holding the doors open while he scanned the room.

About seven or eight cowboys, looking as though they'd been drinking and gambling all night, sat about the cave-dark room. There was only one woman present, sitting at the bar and talking with the apron. They all hushed when they saw Leon, giving him their grim, hostile looks.

It was obvious that, as Stillman had speculated, the Goliad was going to be the toughest nut to crack, the hardest saloon to tame. The problem was it catered mostly to the men who rode for Norman Billingsley, and those who rode for ol' Norman seemed to hold themselves above the law. They thought they could do as they damn well pleased, and if you didn't like it, you'd better be prepared to draw your gun.

That was another thing that made them so canny and arrogant. Most were seasoned gunmen. You could tell by the sharp, soulless eyes and the new-model, well-oiled guns tied low on their thighs.

Shit, Leon carped to himself as he crossed the room, letting the batwings swing shut behind him, and headed for a table.

"Sarsparilla," he called to the barkeep.

"Sarsparilla," one of the gunmen drawled mockingly, just loudly enough for Leon to hear.

Leon turned to the man and flashed his big, white teeth in a grin, nodding his head in greeting. The man wrinkled his bulldog nose at him, and turned back to his card game.

When the girl had brought Leon's sarsparilla, chuffing with amusement, the two men who had been arguing in the far corner of the room started arguing again, softly at first. Their voices built steadily in both volume and fervor, and it was obvious they'd completely forgotten about Leon.

The others in the room watched with amusement, cutting their eyes occasionally to McMannigle, silently daring the new deputy to intervene. Both arguers were obviously feared and respected by their peers, and the spectacle of them fighting was akin to watching two grizzlies sparring over a sow.

Leon sat quietly sipping his sarsparilla and listening to the argument—the picture of innocence.

The two arguers were large and sharp-featured. It was apparent to Leon that they were dull-witted men, cantankerous drunkards who'd made names for themselves by their guns. They gave as little thought to killing as they did to dying. It was a tough life they lived. Only a few made it past thirty. Such men were flotsam, more closely aligned with beasts than civilized men. That's why Leon, for the moment, did not care to get involved. The argument, over some woman in Chinook, did not involve any of the others in the room. And no one else was in immediate danger.

He'd just wait and see what happened. . . .

It wasn't much of a wait. One of the men stood, tossing back his chair. "Stand and draw, goddamn you, Platt!"

The other man hesitated for only a second. Then he, too, stood, releasing the thong over the hammer of his six-shooter. He took three slow steps back, his eyes level with his opponent's. He was trying hard to cover it, but Leon could see that there was a glimmer of fear way back in his bovine eyes.

For a half second, McMannigle shifted his eyes to the others in the room. They were watching him to see what he would do. He intended to do nothing. Why should he? If these men wanted to kill each other, let them kill each other.

"After you, fuck face!" the first man bellowed.

Dead silence. Only the clatter of a dray in the street and the distant bark of a dog.

The first man drew first but the second man beat him to the punch, his gun discharging with a black-powder roar and a burst of flame. The explosion split the silence for an instant and left it more silent than before. The first man staggered, half-turning, and dropped to his knees, the unfired gun in his hand. Blood stained his chest.

"I'll see ya in hell, you sumbitch," he rasped. He fell facedown on the floor with a thump, and died with a jerk and a sigh.

After a long silence, one of the onlookers snickered. The man with the smoking gun turned to him darkly. The man stopped snickering.

Leon cleared his throat. "Holster your gun, friend," he told the killer.

The big, sandy-haired man with a broad, pugnacious face turned to him suddenly, as though just now remembering he was there. "It was a fair fight. He drawed first!"

Leon kept his voice even. "I'm not saying he didn't. Holster your gun."

"You ain't takin' me in."

"Holster your gun," McMannigle said, giving his voice an edge.

"Ain't no nigger takin' me nowhere," the man said softly, staring at Leon with a hard, unwavering gaze.

A smile grew on the man's big, fleshy face. Suddenly, he lifted the gun, crouching. He didn't have time to thumb back the hammer and squeeze the trigger, however. The old Remington that Leon had bought for cheap several years ago and then converted to metallic cartridges barked beneath the table—once, twice, three times. The man staggered back into several chairs, upending a vacant table, leaving his feet, and landing hard on his back with a boom that sent dust up from the cracks between the floorboards.

"Anybody else?" Leon asked the rest of the room.

They were all looking at the second dead man. They turned their eyes back to Leon. Apprehension grew in their faces, a thoughtful sizing up followed by a look that said they didn't like the tally.

Leon shrugged. "Anybody else? To tell you the truth, I'd like to just finish the whole lot o' you right here and now. Prob'ly save me the trouble of doin' it later."

They just looked at him. The apron and the girl at the bar exchanged dark glances, surveyed their other customers, and returned their eyes to Leon. Leon thought he saw a flicker of doubt there, as though maybe, just maybe, he'd put a crack in the toughest nut in town.

He walked over to where the other men were gathered around two tables strewn with empty shot glasses, beer mugs, and playing cards. "You all go home now. Don't let me catch you in town for a couple days, until you've had time to think about how you're gonna act from here on in, when you visit us again."

Leon lifted his hat by the crown, and dropped it back on his head, in a mock farewell gesture. Slowly, glancing at each other and grumbling, the men gathered their cards and cigars and stuffed their money in their pockets. They slid their chairs back, securing their guns in their holsters, and made their way to the door, tossing embittered glances at Leon as they went. Keeping his hand on the six-shooter in his holster, McMannigle watched them go.

When they were all gone and were cursing as they mounted their horses at the hitch rack, he turned to the barman.

"You didn't have to make them leave," the proprietor, Ralph Avery said. "Only two of 'em was causin' trouble. The others were behavin' themselves and drinkin' whiskey—a nickel a glass!"

"Every time trouble erupts in this place," Leon said levelly, "everyone's out. Everyone."

"That ain't fair!"

"That's how it's gonna be—until you stop catering to roughnecks."

Leon turned and headed for the door.

"And what if I don't?" Avery yelled after him.

Leon turned back to the man and shrugged. "You're gonna be just as quiet and peaceful as you are now. You'd better get those bodies hauled out of here before they start to stink."

On the boardwalk, he stood silently staring across the street, where a small crowd had gathered to stare at the saloon. He wondered if these people could see his knees quaking. He hesitated a moment before speaking. He wanted to make sure his voice didn't crack.

"Everything's just hunky-dory," he called, concocting a reassuring smile. "Go on about your business, folks."

But as he turned and made his way down the boardwalk, looking for a place with a free lunch counter, a quiet place where he could get a beer to calm his nerves, he thought that nothing was even close to hunky-dory around here.

Not by by a long shot.

13

Most of the morning, Stillman had been scouring the town for a speckle-gray horse.

He'd found three that fit that description, but none of the owners appeared to be the man who'd shot at him. One, in fact, was a little German lady. She used the horse to pull her spring buggy with a box bed filled with garden produce, which she sold at different locations around town.

Another was an unarmed fourteen-year-old boy who ran errands for local businessmen. The third was a cowboy, but Stillman knew from instinct the man was no gunman. The six-shooter he wore was an old, unconverted, Civil War–model Remington, only good for shooting the occasional rattlesnake. The man carried no rifle, not even a carbine for plugging coyotes.

Worried about Fay, Stillman stopped at the hotel on his way back to the jailhouse. She was dressing in a form-fitting riding habit. He greeted her with a kiss. Aroused, he ran his hand up the back of her thigh and across her taut buttocks.

"Well, this is a nice surprise," she breathed in his ear. She smelled freshly bathed and perfumed. Her hair was down around her shoulders.

He kissed her full lips, ran his hand inside the blouse she hadn't buttoned yet, and over the well-filled corset, opening his hand to give a well-supported breast a healthy squeeze.

"Ben," she complained without heat.

"Goddamn, you're a fine-looking woman."

"You're a fine-looking man. You wanna have some fun? A woman gets lonely around here."

Stillman kissed her again, long and deep. He sighed and pulled away. "I'm on duty."

"What are you doing here, then?"

He sighed, regaining his composure. "It just occurred to me that whoever's after me might try to get at me through you. I just wanted to tell you to be careful today . . . until I can catch this guy."

Fay shook out her hair and began buttoning her blouse. "No luck finding the horse?"

Stillman shook his head and turned to the window. "Not a bit."

"Damn. Well, I'll be careful, Ben. I promise. Don't worry about me."

He turned to her, regarding her riding garb, which she hadn't worn but a few times in Denver, when she'd gone riding with wealthy women who owned horses. "What are your plans for the day?" he asked her, a note of concern in his voice.

"Mrs. McFadden asked me to go riding. I couldn't believe it when she sent her housegirl over this morning. What a dream come true. I've been dying for a ride." She paused, catching the apprehensive look in his stare. "Don't worry, Ben. Iris and I will be together. No one's going to bother the wife of the local banker."

Stillman guessed she was right. Also, his prime suspect in the drygulching was Mr. McFadden himself. Certainly Fay would be safe in the company of the man's wife. Stillman had never met Iris McFadden, but the odds were one in a thousand that she would have any part in her husband's "business" affairs. Besides, Fay seemed to trust her, and that was enough for Stillman.

"Okay," he said with a smile, moving to Fay, taking her shoulders in his hands and kissing her forehead. "Do me a favor and keep your pistol handy, will you?"

Fay turned and walked to the bed, where a small leather holster and cartridge belt lay coiled. She slipped the light, silver-plated five-shooter from the sheath, held it up, and made a show of spinning the cylinder, sticking her tongue earnestly between her lips and squinting her lovely eyes.

"All loaded and ready to go. Pity the rattlesnake, human or otherwise, that crosses my path today."

Chuckling, Stillman kissed her once more and headed for the door. "See ya, Mrs. Stillman."

"See ya, Mr. Stillman."

The jail sat in the middle of First but was separated from both the feed store on its left and the grocery and drugstore on its right by about fifty feet. It had been one of the town's original buildings, a shabby little structure with a patched tin roof and a gallery over the strip of hard-packed clay out front, behind the hitch rack.

An old, brittle office chair sat to the left of the door. There was no boardwalk. "Hill County Sheriff" had been printed in gold-leafed letters on the hovel's only window.

Inside, the office was separated from the cells by a plank door. A wood stove sat in the middle of the room. There was a rolltop desk, a swivel office chair on coast-ers, two hide-bottom chairs before the window, and a gun rack bearing three rifles secured by a chain and a padlock. Three curled, yellowed wanted dodgers were tacked to a bulletin board on the wall opposite the desk.

Stillman had come in early this morning and swept the place out, hauled all the wool blankets from the cell block to a laundress, and oiled the swivel chair before the desk. He'd tapped the tin chimney pipe running along the ceiling to the wall, and noted it needed taking apart and cleaning, lest his first fire of the cold season smoke him out.

On his way over from the hotel, he'd stopped at a gunsmith shop and picked up several boxes of ammunition. He was dumping them in a desk drawer when his sole prisoner, the man who'd tried ventilating his poker partner last night and then slugged Leon in the kisser, began rattling his coffee cup against the bars of his cell.

Stillman crossed the room and opened the plank door leading back to the cells.

"What do you want?"

"Let me out o' here, Sheriff," the man wheedled. "I'm sorry. Honest to god, I am. I didn't want to shoot ol' Jory. I was just crazy drunk, that's all."

"Tell that to the judge."

Stillman was about to shut the door against the prisoner's continuing protests. He stopped, hesitated, and scowled. "Oh, all right, all right," he groused, grabbing the key off the wall peg and heading down the corridor between the cells, two on each side of the alley.

"I'm gonna let you go on your own recognizance— mostly because I'm not gonna be in town to feed you at noon and Leon's got his hands full with the rest of

the town. But so help me god, Cliff, if you ever dis-
charge your weapon in this town again, I'm gonna lock
you up and talk the judge into throwing away the key!"

The prisoner licked his lips and widened his eyes as
he watched Stillman unlock the door. "Oh, thank you,
Sheriff. Thank you. Bless you." He was nearly crying.
"I don't know what got into me—I really don't. But I'll
be good. I promise I will."

Stillman drew the door wide. "Get out of here."

"Bless you, Sheriff. Bless you. I'm gonna go right
back out to the ranch and apologize to ol' Jory and get
right back to work stretchin' fence for Mr. Tinglehoff.
He only has me and Jory on his role this summer, you
know, so he's purty short-handed, and . . . well . . . don't
you worry. You prob'ly won't see me again till fall!"

"That's too soon for me," Stillman yelled at him, as
he followed the man into the office and watched him
hightail it out the door.

The door did not shut behind him. It was grabbed by
someone else. Two men filed in—Bernard McFadden in
his customarily high-toned duds, and Judge Humperdink, who looked characteristically grandfatherly with
his long, white beard and the gold fob chain arcing from
a pocket of his black waistcoat.

Stillman was about to greet both men, but before he
could speak, McFadden stopped near the wood stove and
yelled, "What in the hell do you think you're doing,
Sheriff?" His face was red with anger. Spittle jetted from
his lips. The judge walked up to flank him, frowning
with the air of a man on a necessary but distasteful mis-
sion.

"Good morning to you, too," Stillman said wryly, caught off guard by the man's anger.

"Don't give me any wisecracks, you maniac! What in the hell is the meaning of this?" McFadden stomped over to the desk and slammed down two invoices. "In your first twenty-four hours as sheriff, you've run up a bill of sixty-five dollars! One for a window and one for two dead horses!"

Stillman shrugged, at a loss for what to say. He had to admit it sounded a little extreme. "Well . . ."

"And this morning I heard from Doc Evans that you killed another man—old man Andrews. I thought you were going to deliver the bodies so he could bury them, not *kill him,* too!"

"Well . . ."

"And according to Mr. Billingsley, you beat up two of his men over at Sam Wah's. Tossed one through the window. Never mind that they had nothing to do with Daryl Bruner's death. You wanted to send a message out to *Norman*!"

Stillman was feeling bleak. All he could say was another "Well . . ."

"And to top it all off, your deputy—that black man—just shot a man over in the Goliad!"

"Leon . . . ?" Stillman said, perking up with sudden concern.

"Is that his name? You certainly never informed the council you were hiring a Negro."

"I didn't know it mattered. Is he all right?"

"Oh, he's fine," McFadden continued, looking as though a stroke were imminent. "He's over having a beer and a free lunch just down the street while Ralph

Avery's drawing up another bill for the damage done to his saloon!"

Stillman was mad now, too. "You can tell Ralph Avery to kiss my ass! If you pay his bill, you're nuts. He caters to a troublemaking crowd. As for the rest of it, nothing I did was in any way, shape, or form outside the law. The two men in Sam Wah's started the fight and I defended myself. Old man Andrews pulled a gun and I shot him. Then some bastard on a speckle-gray horse tried to bushwack me on my way back to town. When I find that son of a bitch, you're probably going to have another bill—for the ten pounds of ammunition I expend taking him down!"

There was a heavy pause. The judge surveyed Stillman judiciously. McFadden dropped his chin to regard Stillman from under his pewter brows. "How dare you raise your voice to me," he said tightly.

Stillman leaned over the desk, planting his fists on the invoices and looking up at the banker, who resembled nothing less than an old locomotive chugging up a mountain.

"You don't seem to understand, McFadden. There's a certain price every town has to pay for justice. If you don't want to pay it, you best send me on my way and bring in another career cowboy—someone you can wrap around your little finger and use to your best advantage, then throw away when he gets too big for his britches." This last had steamed out of Stillman involuntarily. He hadn't wanted to inform McFadden he suspected him of Ralph Merchant's murder, but his anger had gotten away from him.

"That can be arranged," McFadden growled. A darkness had crept into his angry gaze, as though he were now entertaining more thoughts than those he'd come with.

"Okay, gentlemen, that's enough," the judge intervened, moving up to position himself between the two men. "You have to admit, Mr. Stillman, it all does sound a little extreme. And the way you're treating Norman Billingsley, a very respected businessman . . ."

"If he doesn't send Rafe Paul to me, I'm going to go out there and arrest him for harboring a fugitive."

The old graybeard raised his eyebrows sternly, like a grandfather speaking to a stubborn child. "We have little evidence that's the case. Norman rode into town yesterday, while you were out at the Andrews place, and informed me that Rafe Paul had shot young Bruner, god rest the poor boy's soul, in self-defense. The five men he had with him, who had witnessed the disturbance, all vouched for Mr. Paul."

Stillman sighed with disgust and straightened, crossing his arms over his chest. "Judge, why would Bruner want to start a fight with Rafe Paul? From what I heard from Jody and Crystal Harmon, he was a mild-mannered idiot."

"With a temper," the judge added. "Especially when it came to animals. Apparently Paul had kicked a cat in the saloon. Daryl was known for raising the roof when he saw anyone mistreating an animal. Why, he even ran up to me one day and scolded me for whipping my buggy horse!"

The judge paused, catching his breath. "When Paul kicked the cat, Daryl grew so hot that he borrowed a gun and called Paul out in the street."

"I don't believe it, Judge," Stillman said. "Jody said the boy didn't even know how to fire a gun. Crystal said he was goaded into the fight, and that the gun was forced on him."

"I thought she didn't see the actual shooting."

"She didn't—someone busted her in the chops—but she saw everything that led up to it."

"That's not enough," the judge said, shaking his head.

"I'm bringing Paul in," Stillman told him. "I've already written out the warrant. We can hear his story, and Crystal's story, at the hearing."

"Don't do it, Stillman," McFadden warned. He'd composed himself and taken a subsidiary stance behind and to the right of the judge, apparently satisfied with the way Humperdink was proceeding.

"You two are pretty tight with this Billingsley, I take it," Stillman said, with a wry humor.

McFadden said, "He's put a lot of money into this town, Stillman."

The judge interceded. "I cannot deny that Bernard, Norman, and I are friends . . . and business associates. But I am first and foremost judge of Hill County, and if I thought we had a clear-cut case against Rafe Paul, I would certainly tell you to go ahead and bring him in. But since we don't, I see no reason to ruffle Norman's feathers. Paul is his ramrod—a good man. He came up the Texas trail with Norman a year and a half ago, and he's helped Norman establish himself as the biggest rancher in Hill County." He added with a smile, apparently trying to lighten the conversation, "And his house isn't even finished yet!"

"His men frequent the Goliad," Stillman said. "And

from what I've heard—and seen—they're the prime troublemakers around town. They're the reason you called me in."

"Yes . . . ," the judge said, hesitating, trying to find the right words. "But to settle them down a little . . . maybe lock the particularly bad ones up for a day or two . . . but not—"

"But not lay down any real rules that would ruffle Norman's feathers."

McFadden said, "Our real problem is with the gamblers and the damn Indians and transients and with the penny-ante outlaws that hole up in the Two Bears. *They're* who you and your . . . your *deputy* should be focusing on."

"You know, I never heard of a town with two sets of laws," Stillman said with another wry chuckle. "This is a first for me. And here I thought you were just afraid of vigilantes. You're not afraid of vigilantes. You're afraid of any *real* law enforcement."

The judge waved his wrinkled, old paw. "That's not true, Stillman."

"Bullshit."

"*Mister* Stillman."

"You know what, though?" Stillman continued. "I have a feelin' you two are in the minority around here. I have a feelin' that most of the good citizens of Clantick want the whole town cleaned up, not just the part not associated with Norman Billingsley. If I'm wrong, I'm out of here. But I have a feeling I'm right. And I have a feeling that part of my cleaning up this town is getting you two old fence-straddlers and pocket liners off your high horses, and run out of town with the rest of the penny-ante criminals . . . on a *rail*!"

Stillman's visitors had been cowed into sheepish, angry silence. They glanced at each other, as if unsure how to proceed. Finally McFadden brushed past the judge toward Stillman. "You're going to regret those words, you old fossil," he growled through clenched teeth.

Then, turning to the judge, he said, "Come on, Charles. There's obviously no reasoning with this man." He slapped his hat on his head and headed for the door. The judge stood glaring a moment longer at Stillman, then turned and followed him. At the door he stopped and half-turned, giving his old eyes to Stillman one last time. "If you bring Rafe Paul in—and that's a big if— I'll throw the case out of court."

Then he and McFadden were gone.

Stillman stood staring at the door, his mind storming with disconnected thoughts propelled by sheer adrenaline.

The door opened again a moment later. Doc Evans ducked his head in, a spirited grin spreading his big, red mustache. A smoking stogey poked out from his mouth.

"What do you want?" Stillman growled, still angry at his previous visitors.

Unperturbed, the doctor shut the door behind him and sauntered into the room. He jerked a thumb over his shoulder. "I heard it. Most of it, anyway." He shrugged his rounded shoulders beneath his pin-striped, collarless shirt and ragged vest. His derby was dented. Stillman thought he'd been drinking.

"And?"

Evans's grin widened. "I think they wish they hadn't

killed Ralph Merchant. They hadn't figured on Jody Harmon suggesting they bring you in, and the other councilmen going for it." He chuckled with unabashed delight.

"What about you?" Stillman asked, cocking an eye at the man.

"Me?" the doctor chuckled. "Hell, I couldn't be happier. Business has never been better!"

"Well, it's nice to see someone's pleased." Stillman indicated a chair. "Have a seat."

The doctor shook his head. "Can't stay. I just stopped by to say hi and to tell you to keep the patients and cadavers coming. At this rate I'll be able to pay my bill over at the Drovers in two weeks!"

He lifted a hand to scratch the back of his head, adding, "But I have a feeling if you and your deputy keep going the way you're going, I'm going to be laying the two of you out soon."

"Well, if that's all you have, I'll be excusing myself," Stillman said, heading for the wall peg where his hat hung. He donned the ten-gallon Stetson and looked at the doctor. "I've got business out at Billingsley's. You wouldn't draw me a map, would you?"

The doctor found a pencil on the desk. He turned over a paper scrap and began a hurried sketch. "Just follow the freight road north of town about seven miles. Take a left at Judson's Store—it's an old trading post—and follow the trail into that valley. There was a horse trail last time I was out there; it's probably a full-blown wagon road by now. You'll see the house ol' Norman's building up on the ridge to your right, about two miles west of the store."

Stillman took the paper from the doctor's outstretched hand. "Much obliged," he said, grabbing his Henry and opening the door.

Evans shook his head. "Don't thank me. If you follow that map, it might be the last map you'll ever follow." His look was dark.

Stillman glanced at him, then went out and shut the door.

14

When Fay had finished getting into her habit, with its rather confining corset, she wrapped the gun and holster around her waist and cinched the belt. Snugging her felt riding hat on her head and straightening the bun which she'd coiled and secured with a whalebone barrette her grandmother had passed down to her, she headed out the door.

Iris McFadden was waiting for her outside, decked out in an olive green habit with a straw bonnet and calfskin gloves. She was an intense-looking woman, with high, wide cheekbones stretched above a rather pert, old world mouth. Her blond hair was flecked with gray, and her brown eyes, stretched as they were above those chiseled, almost Indian-like facial bones, were enormous.

She had a nervous, somewhat cunning smile, and her actions seemed overdone, as if she was always a little overwrought. But Fay liked the woman for the simple, obvious reason that Iris seemed to like Fay, and had gone right to work making Fay feel at home here in Clantick. Beneath a rather thick veneer, Fay sensed a vulnerability, and Fay had always been attracted to vulnerable people.

Before they'd exchanged greetings this morning, however, Fay stopped short on the hotel's veranda, the white-painted doors closing behind her. Her heart quickened as she stared at the horse upon which Mrs. McFadden rode. The horse regarded her unseeing as it jerked its head and stretched its lips away from its teeth, adjusting the bit.

"Something wrong, dear?" Iris McFadden inquired, her greeting smile still stretching her thin, painted lips.

Fay tried to compose herself as she moved down the steps, lifting the skirt of her habit above her ankles. "No . . . not at all," she said. "I just . . . what a nice horse you have there. I love speckle-grays."

"Yes, old Tom's a handsome boy. I've had him for years, ride him nearly everywhere he'll take me. Used to be quite a runner in his day, but now he prefers more of a bridle-path stroll. He'll be fifteen years old next month."

She regarded the horse which one of her houseboys was holding beside the speckle-gray. "I thought you'd look lovely against the stallion, your hair being black, so I had Rodney saddle him for you this morning. Bernard calls him Star."

Thoughts whirling, Fay had trouble taking her eyes off the speckle-gray. She wondered if Iris could tell something was bothering her. She knew her face must have flushed stove-red. Inwardly commanding herself to settle down, and telling herself there must be at least fifty speckle-gray horses in town, she managed a smile and turned to the black. She ran her hands down the animal's fine neck, cooing to the horse, saying its name, letting it get to know her.

"You're a fine-looking boy," Fay said as the animal turned its head to her, gently nibbling her habit and sniffing her loudly. She pulled a sugar cube she'd swiped from her breakfast table, and showed it to Iris. "May I?"

"Go ahead, dear. He'd love it. I can tell he's already falling for you."

Mrs. McFadden laughed with delight. She had a husky, uninhibited laugh, which Fay liked. Iris was married to a society gentleman, but she was no run-of-the-mill society lady. She had character, a strong sense of her own being, and did not mind expressing it. Unlike so many women Fay had known, she did not define herself solely by whom she'd married.

When the horse had eaten the cube, Fay grabbed the horn, poked her boot through the stirrup, and mounted up, enjoying the feel of the leather beneath her again, and accepted the reins from the houseboy.

"Come on, my good Star," she said gently, reining the horse away from the hitching post, taking Iris's lead. "I haven't been on a horse in a while, so you'll have patience with me, won't you? Okay . . . here we go."

Five minutes later they were cantering, stirrup to stirrup, on the wagon road south of town, heading toward the Two Bear Mountains, dark and distant under a flawless summer sky. Fay had put her concern over the speckle-gray out of her mind. The horse belonged to Iris, not her husband. If Mr. McFadden had wanted to bushwack Ben, he would not have ridden Iris's old Tom. In fact, he probably wouldn't have ridden any of the horses in his own stable.

No, Fay told herself. Neither Iris nor her horse had had anything to do with bushwacking Ben.

"You seem very much at home on a horse," Iris observed as they cantered down the lane, gophers scuttling out of their way and chortling at them from holes pocking the prairie.

"I grew up with horses," Fay said with a thoughtful smile, recalling her years growing up along the banks of the Yellowstone River, near Milestown. She'd been an only child, and had countered the loneliness of growing up in a remote place, isolated from other children, by reading every book she could find and exploring the country on horseback, concocting rich fantasies while she rode.

"Yes, I remember you mentioning that yesterday over tea. That's why I thought you'd like a ride."

"Iris, I can't thank you enough," Fay told her, genuinely grateful for the woman's thoughtfulness.

"Oh, please, dear," Iris said self-effacingly. "You don't know how nice it is to finally have a woman in town with my . . . tastes, if you will."

"Tastes?"

"Yes . . . well . . . a woman who doesn't mind getting her clothes dirty . . . or leaving town for a few hours' ride in the country. That sort of thing. Most of the women in Clantick, I'm afraid, are rather stodgy little things, cowering behind their curtains all day, waiting for their husbands to come home so they can cook for them and get told how beautiful they are." Iris flushed and glanced at Fay with a look of embarrassment. "Oh, dear, there I go again, on one of my tirades."

"No, I understand," Fay said. "I'm afraid that's how my first husband wanted things. You've probably heard about him; he was infamous around here. But Ben and I . . . we don't try to rein each other in. I guess we both understand that the only way a marriage can truly work is if there's a certain amount of freedom." She shrugged.

"Yes," Iris said, when they'd directed their horses off the road to let a ranch wagon pass, the driver tipping his hat and bidding them good day. "Bernard and I have come to a certain understanding about"—she hesitated, "freedom."

The morning waned. The women loped their horses and rested them in a box elder grove, talking easily, with greater and greater abandon. By noon they'd ridden into the mountains, branching off the wagon trail to follow a deer path through woods and glens where cattle grazed, frisky spring calves playing close to their mothers.

Heading eastward, they came to a valley through which a creek wended its way between a pine-clad mountain on one side and a grassy, wildflower-carpeted slope climbing to a rocky ridge on the other. Far above the ridge, two golden eagles hunted, giving their periodic cries, their shadows flickering about the rocks.

When the women came to a shady aspen grove, Iris reined her horse to a halt.

"What do you say we picnic here?"

"Oh, I was hoping you'd thought of lunch," Fay said. "I'm famished!"

When they'd tethered their horses in the aspens and loosened their saddles, Iris removed her saddlebags from the rump of her speckle-gray, and led Fay down to the creek, shaded on one side by the trees. The air was cool and fresh near the water, and moss grew on the rocks. The grass was rich and green and bowed with moisture.

Fay helped Iris spread a picnic blanket. Iris dug into

her saddlebags, producing sandwiches, dates, fruit, and a bottle of wine.

"You went all out," Fay exclaimed.

"Oh, it's only some roast beef left over from last night, I'm afraid. It's probably fairly dry by now."

"Riding makes me hungry."

"Here, dig into one of these. Wine?"

"Why not?" Fay said with an obliging chuckle, remembering the time, two years ago, when she and Ben had picnicked in these very mountains and shared a bottle of wine, as they'd done down on the Yellowstone, the first time they'd ridden together.

"So . . . how do you like Clantick so far?" Iris asked her while they ate, sitting facing the creek, their hats resting at their sides, wineglasses clutched in their hands.

Fay shrugged. "To be honest, it's a little rougher than I expected. Someone tried to shoot Ben yesterday. Did you hear?"

Iris mumbled something.

"Pardon?" Fay asked, turning to her and frowning.

Iris shrugged and smiled innocently. "I just said that's to be expected, isn't it? I mean a new sheriff in a new town . . . being a little *zealous,* if what I heard is true." She giggled self-consciously.

"Zealous?" Fay said, incredulous. It was the first time Iris had said anything that put her off, and Fay was puzzled.

Iris turned her head to stare at the creek, her face coloring a little. She brought her knees up to her chest and hugged them. "Bernard told me that he'd thrown a man through the window at Sam Wah's . . . which seems, for his first day on the job . . . a little . . . *dramatic*—doesn't it, Fay?"

She turned her head to Fay, and her eyes were mildly beseeching, wrinkled at the corners.

Fay thought about it, trying not to let her emotions get away from her. It wasn't easy. "I suppose it might have seemed a little . . . *drastic,* but if Ben got into a scuffle with those men, you can be sure he wasn't the one who instigated it."

Iris's eyes turned at once sweet and remorseful. She tipped her head and squinted her eyes, shaking her head. "You know what, Fay?" she said, pausing meaningfully. "I had no right to say that to you."

Fay studied the woman's apologetic eyes, a little perplexed by the sudden change of heart. Iris was definitely a woman it took some getting to know. She was downright odd, in fact, but Fay had always prided herself on her acceptance, even her delight, in the oddities of others. They gave life color, after all. Wanting very much for Iris to be her friend, Fay was looking for any reason not to get angry.

She shrugged. "That's all right, Iris."

"Really, Fay? Because I really am sorry. I don't know what got into me, making such a judgment. I had no right whatsoever, and you know what's more? I don't even know if it's true."

Fay narrowed her gaze, unsure what Iris had meant by that last sentence. She assumed she'd meant that her information had been filtered by Mr. McFadden. "I guess our husbands haven't exactly become fast friends, have they?"

Iris put a sisterly hand on Fay's knee and squeezed.

"No, they haven't," she agreed, still gazing deeply into Fay's eyes. "But that has nothing to do with us. If those two want to fight over who controls the town, then I say let them fight. It shouldn't affect us a bit. They have their lives and we have ours."

"I agree."

"It's settled then?"

"Settled."

Iris offered her hand. "Shake?"

Fay shook it, feeling a little self-conscious.

Iris said, "Now what do you say we let our hair down a little."

"What's that?"

"Here . . . turn your back to me."

"I'm sorry . . . I don't . . ."

"I'm going to loosen your bun and let that gorgeous hair down. You know, if I had hair like that, I certainly wouldn't be wearing it up. I'd let it caress my shoulders all day long!"

Iris put her hands on Fay's shoulders, turned Fay's back to her, and went to work on the bun. In a minute, Fay's chocolate curls were falling down her back.

"There . . . now doesn't that feel better?"

Fay smiled nervously. "Yeah, I guess it does," she said, shaking her head and taking the whalebone barrette from Iris. She felt uncomfortable with the woman's intimate contact, usually reserved for sisters and longtime friends, but she played along. What had been the point of wearing her hair up so tightly, anyway? It certainly felt better loose than all knotted up on her head.

"Do mine, will you, Fay?" Iris said, offering her back.

"Sure . . . Iris . . . of course . . . ," Fay said, again feeling funny.

The woman's gray-streaked blond hair fell thickly around her shoulders, and Iris swung her head, cooing with satisfaction. "Oh, that feels good!" She reached for the bottle and turned to Fay. "More wine?"

Fay lifted her glass. "Why not?" She really didn't want more; the first glass, coupled with the sound of running water, the summer warmth, and the bright sun dimpling the creek and reflecting off the tawny grass of the opposite slope, had made her woozy. But she didn't want to spoil Iris's fun.

As the two women sipped their wine, they talked of common things—the best shops to find certain things around Clantick, where Fay might find a horse to buy, a book group that met once a month in the Lutheran parsonage—and Fay felt herself growing more at ease. Finally they sank back on the blanket, enjoying the sun on their faces and the caress of the breeze, falling silent to listen to the rattle of the leaves and the water. Fay finished her wine, set down her glass, and closed her eyes.

She didn't know how long she'd dozed before she felt something on her check. She turned her head and opened her eyes. For a moment, she thought she must be dreaming. She blinked several times, trying to clear the fog from her brain.

After several seconds she realized she was awake, and it was true—Iris McFadden was caressing her face.

15

Fay lifted her head. "Iris . . . !"

Iris smiled, rolled onto her back, and stretched her arms above her head. "Oh, don't be embarrassed, dear. I just wanted to touch you."

Fay gaped at her in shock.

"It just takes some getting used to, dear." Iris rolled toward Fay, coming to rest on her belly. She propped herself up on her elbows. She lifted her feet and crossed them at the ankles, girlishly. When she spoke again, her voice was soft and throaty. "You're lovely."

Fay turned to her angrily, searching for the words.

"Oh, don't get riled," Iris gently chided.

Fay sat up and slid several inches away from the woman as she turned to face her, tossing her hair from her eyes with a derisive sweep of her hand. "Look," she said, her voice shaking a little as she tried to maintain control, "I don't know what you're doing, Iris, but—"

"Oh, I think you know," the woman said casually. Yet Fay could see a deep blush creeping up from her neck. "Isn't it obvious?"

Fay stared at the woman in shocked disbelief. She didn't know what to say. She'd never been confronted this way before . . . by a woman.

She tried to swallow her anger and maintain reason, an objective equanimity. "Iris," she tried, paused, and tried again. "I'm sorry if I gave you . . . signals that might have led you to believe—"

Iris's face fell, crestfallen. Fay's expression softened as she suddenly felt she understood the woman. She pitied her, was embarrassed for her. How much of her life had been given to this kind of solicitation, only to have it rejected, over and over again?

"I'm sorry, Iris. I . . . I don't know what to say."

"That's okay," the woman said, slowly climbing to her feet, looking away. Her face was flushed with embarrassment. "Just give me a moment please. I'd like to compose myself."

When she had drifted off in the trees, Fay sat there for several minutes, feeling mortified for the woman, wishing she could go back in time and fix it so none of it had happened. How would she and Iris ever be able to speak to each other again? How would they ever be able to look at each other again? It was a heavy, nagging sadness in Fay's heart; she felt she'd made a friend and just as quickly lost her. She felt guilty, as though the fault were hers.

Finally, she gathered the remaining food and eating utensils, and packed them and the picnic cloth in Iris's saddlebags. Carrying the bags to the speckle-gray, she saw for the first time that the saddle boot attached to Iris's saddle contained a rifle. Fay remembered Ben saying that the rifle shells he had found, left behind by whoever had ambushed him, had belonged to a Springfield.

Fay's heart lurched suddenly with a stab of suspicion. She felt ashamed for what she was thinking, but her urge to see the gun was undeniable. She glanced furtively at the trees where Iris had disappeared. Hands shaking, she grasped the walnut stock and pulled the heavy rifle from the sheath. She knew enough about rifles to know that their manufacturers often stamped their makes and calibers somewhere on the barrel or receiver. This one was stamped on the barrel, about six inches from the hammer.

The gun was a .45–70 Springfield. Fay's breath caught in her throat. The hair prickled on the nape of her neck. She slid the rifle back in its sheath, telling herself that Springfield was a common make. But another part of her knew that the rifle coupled with the speckle-gray horse was too much of a coincidence. This had to be the horse belonging to the person who'd ambushed Ben, and this had to be the rifle he—or she—had used.

Fay turned the problem over in her mind. It had to have been Iris's husband who'd ambushed Ben . . . or Iris herself.

But why? What possible reason could either of them have for wanting Ben dead? He'd come to save their town.

"What's the matter, Fay? You look as though you've seen a ghost."

Fay wheeled. Iris stood directly behind her, a big, insolent smile on her face. She was now fully dressed. She was wearing her straw riding hat with a tuft of fresh flowers pinned to the low crown. Before Fay realized what the woman was doing, Iris reached forward and grabbed the nickel-plated revolver out of Fay's holster.

Aiming the .35-caliber weapon at Fay's belly, Iris thumbed back the hammer.

Heart pounding wildly, Fay stumbled backward against the horse. "It . . . was . . . you. . . . You ambushed Ben. . . ."

Iris gave a little movement with her shoulders. "He would have found out."

"Found out . . ."

". . . about me and my less than orthodox appetite for tender young lovelies like yourself, Mrs. Stillman."

Fay shook her head, uncomprehendingly. "*What?* Why would Ben care that you . . .?"

". . . killed a few of Clantick's quote unquote 'daughters of joy'?"

"*You* killed those women?"

"I shouldn't say I *killed* them." Iris paused thoughtfully, apparently unsure whether she should continue. Fay felt as though she could read the woman's mind. What would talking about it matter? Fay would be dead soon. Besides, talking about it was like scratching a chronic itch. She couldn't help herself.

"Some of them couldn't take it when I got aroused. I didn't *kill* them. But that's how your husband would have seen it. That's how Ralph Merchant saw it, when he found out. Bernard was kind enough to hire a couple of Norman Billingsley's men to follow him and Bernard out from town on one of their hunting trips, and lynch Ralph Merchant, to make it look like Indians getting back at the town for lynching one of their own."

"Oh my god, it was you . . . both of you. Your husband knows."

Iris cackled with delight. "He's not my husband, Fay. He's my *brother*!" This, too, Iris apparently wanted to get off her chest, to share with at least one other person, so they could see how brilliantly evil she was.

Fay just looked at her, then glanced at the gun aimed at her middle.

"We came from the East, from a rather close, affluent family," Iris continued, conversationally, almost as though she were talking to herself. "I couldn't marry . . . for obvious reasons . . . and Bernard . . . well, Bernard maintains he's a born bachelor, but I have a feeling he's . . ." She let the sentence trail off.

"Let me put it this way. Our parents died, Bernard's and mine, and Bernard wanted to head west, where our father had already made a fortune in speculations without having stepped one foot across the Mississippi. The fortune was half mine, and I wanted to come, too. The East can be so . . . so . . . confining, if you know what I mean. Well, the easiest way for us to travel and not have to answer a bunch of questions about why neither of us had married was to feign we *were* married . . . to each other." Her facial features cooled, and for the first time Fay saw pure, unmitigated evil in the woman's eyes. "Who out here would know?" She laughed her brittle, hackneyed laugh, and leaned closer to Fay.

"Get away from me!" Fay said, her voice quaking with anger, as she turned and headed for her horse.

Iris grabbed her shoulder, turned her back around, and slapped her once, hard, in the face. Fay reeled, stunned.

She regained her senses, drew back her arm, and, with an angry cry, swung her clenched fist against Iris's jaw. Iris gave a grunt and staggered, reaching out for the horse to steady herself. She brought the gun to bear, aiming it at Fay's face. "I'm gonna hurt you for that . . . before I kill you. Get on your horse."

"Why?"

"Because I don't want to haul your dead body to where I'm going to dump you. You're going to ride there." She pursed her lips with self-satisfaction. "Then I'll kill you."

"I'm not going anywhere with you. If you're going to kill me, you're going to have to do it here."

Iris acquired a fond, dreamy look. "The whores," Iris said, reaching out to touch the hair hanging along Fay's cheek. "None of them were as lovely as you. They provided . . . entertainment . . . for a while. The problem with them was that, in spite of their tough occupation, they weren't really very tough women. They didn't hold up well. You would have held up well enough. You can give it back as well as you can take it, can't you, dear?"

Fay's anger became a thick, frothy substance within her. "You've got that right, Iris," she said. And with a sudden swing of her left hand, catching Mrs. McFadden completely off guard, she knocked the gun out of her hand. The gun barked as it arced off in the grass. Without waiting for Iris's reaction, she smashed her right fist against the woman's jaw. Iris went down hard, sprawling in the grass and frightening both horses, crab-stepping against their tethered reins.

Shocked, Iris brought her hand to her bloody lip, inspected the blood smeared on her knuckles. She was looking around for Fay's gun just as Fay bent to retrieve it. Fay squared her shoulders, a hard look in her eyes, and brought the gun to her shoulder.

Iris regarded her, chest heaving with anger. "You pack a good punch, Mrs. Stillman. But I don't think you can shoot me."

"Don't tempt me, Iris."

Iris pushed herself awkwardly to her feet. She glanced at the speckle-gray to her right. Fay read her mind. "Iris . . . ," she warned.

It fell on deaf ears. Iris reached for the rifle, slid it smoothly out of its sheath.

"Iris, I'm warning you!" Fay yelled.

It, too, fell on deaf ears.

Iris brought the heavy gun to her shoulder, pulling back the hammer. The barrel was swinging toward Fay in a deadly arc.

Fay squeezed the trigger of her .35, and the gun gave a sharp crack, spitting smoke and fire, jogging her wrist. The bullet tore into Iris's shoulder.

"You bitch!" Iris screamed, reeling sideways with the impact of the bullet and the weight of the gun in her arms. She caught her balance and again swung the rifle around toward Fay. Both horses were screaming and pulling at their reins. Blackbirds were cawing and thundering from the trees.

Fay sighted down the short barrel of her Smith & Wesson, held her breath, and squeezed off another round. This one was for keeps. Iris staggered backward, eyes rolling up into her head, and fell on her butt. She sat with her legs spread, rifle dangling between her legs, then collapsed backward in the grass. Blood trickled through the penny-sized hole in her left temple.

Slowly, Fay lowered the pistol to her side. She gave a shudder.

"If you say so, Iris."

16

Earlier that morning, Bob Andrews sat on the loafer's bench outside the grocery store fifty yards west of the jailhouse. Hat pulled low over his eyes, he ran his knife down the chunk of cottonwood in his hand, adding another curl of the green wood to the small pile between his feet, furtively cutting his eyes to the jailhouse on his left. He brought them back to the wood and stuck his tongue out as he worked, feigning concentration.

Just another innocent loafer killing time.

The door behind Bob opened and a middle-aged woman and a girl of about sixteen stepped onto the boardwalk. Both wore fashionable suits with feathered hats and cameo pins fastening ruffled blouses closed at their throats. Their perfume wafted thickly in the morning breeze, nearly making Bob's eyes water.

He smiled and nodded at the two women—just a harmless loafer loafing away the morning in front of Harrison's Grocery & Drug Store, bidding the ladies good day with a pinch of the old hat brim. The woman and the girl glanced at him, measuring his scruffy countenance, his unwashed clothes and unshaven cheeks, and turned up their noses, averting their eyes. Lifting their skirts, they marched haughtily down the steps to the street.

Bob had wanted to sit here as inconspicuously as possible, but his anger burned up from his middle and quickened his pulse. This was the thanks he got for trying to act decent, for greeting these ladies like a gentleman. That's the way it was with the rich. If you didn't wear a twenty-dollar suit and a silk top hat, you weren't good enough to greet on the street. And they wonder why they get robbed!

"Hey, old lady—ask your daughter if she'd sit on my face for a while." Bob asked the woman, voice teeming with raw insolence.

The woman turned to him sharply, opening her mouth to say something. She stopped herself, turned to the girl, said, "Come along, Franci," and climbed into the red-wheeled buggy parked at the hitch rack.

"Come here and climb on my lap, Franci," Bob said, giving his thigh a slap.

Climbing into the jitney, the girl glanced at him horrified.

Bob stuck out his tongue and made a licking gesture. The girl turned away, wide-eyed with horror.

"Don't look at him, Franci. That's what he wants you to do," the woman said. Stiffly, chin up, face flushed, she unwrapped the reins from the brake and clucked to the Thoroughbred in the traces. "Gidup, Pierre!"

"Does that mean no?" Bob called after them.

He settled back on the bench and chuckled to himself. Then, when the thrill was gone, he chided himself. They could have gone to the sheriff and reported his bad behavior. That would have put Bob in a hell of a fix. He was growing whiskers to try and disguise himself, but what if the new sheriff recognized him, anyway? He'd be behind bars with little or no hope of settling the score with the man, whose name he'd learned was Stillman. Ben Stillman, deputy U.S. marshal, retired.

The name caused adrenaline to spurt in Bob's veins. His heart bounced with fear. He'd heard of Stillman, as practically everyone in the territory had at one time or another. Bob had thought Stillman was out of commission, however. It was just Bob's luck that he'd shown up here, on the very same train Bob and his brother and cousins had been trying to rob!

Now Bob had to try and kill the son of a bitch—or face his father. Bob wasn't sure which was worse. He only knew what he had to do. The thought going down like camphor, he glanced again at the jail.

He'd been watching the building for the past hour. It was a busy place, two men in fancy suits having stormed in about twenty minutes ago. They'd yelled themselves hoarse before storming out, climbing onto their horses, and riding off. As they'd been coming out, another man had gone in—a stocky, broad-shouldered gent dressed more like a whiskey drummer than the doctor Bob knew him to be. Bob wished the doctor would come back out now, so he could mosey over and do what he had to do before he lost his nerve.

The best way to handle it, he figured, was to stroll in looking harmless, pull out his gun, and plug Stillman before the lawman even knew what was happening. He'd read about someone doing that to the sheriff over in Shelby, and getting away with it.

The jailhouse door clicked. Bob turned toward it, expecting to see the stocky, red-whiskered doctor walk out. His mouth dried with fear and disappointment when he saw that the person leaving the jail was Ben Stillman himself.

Goddamn . . .

Bob froze there in his chair, not sure what to do. He dropped his eyes and made some halfhearted attempts at whittling the stick. Then he turned his head slightly, stealing a look at the lawman from under his hat brim.

Stillman paused at the hitch rack to place his rifle under his arm and light a long-nine cigar, cupping the match in his hands and puffing smoke. He wagged out the lucifer, took the rifle in his right hand, and headed kitty-corner across the street, for the boardwalk directly across from Bob. Stillman strolled down the boardwalk, string tie blowing, corduroy jacket flapping open. He tipped his head to two young ladies heading his way sporting parasols. They beamed at him shyly and dropped their eyes, then turned to glance at his back. One giggled and covered her mouth. The other admonished her with a sharp look and words Bob couldn't hear.

Stillman turned the first corner he came to, and disappeared down a side street, past a barbershop where a shaggy dog with collie spots slept under the hitch rack, chin on its crossed front paws. Just like that, Stillman was gone. And here sat Bob, looking bereft, holding the knife and stick in his idle hands.

Goddamnit.

Bob looked at the wood, scowling, as if suddenly finding a horse turd in his lap. He tossed the wood in the street, stood, and sheathed his knife on his hip. He cursed again, kicked the coffee can the loafers used for a spittoon, and marched westward along the boardwalk.

His plans were ruined, and he didn't have a backup.

He was half-glad. He didn't feel up to shooting Still-man today. He'd wait for another day, and he'd plan ahead. This morning he'd walked uptown for a bath and, remembering the newspaper story he'd read about the sheriff getting shot in his Shelby office, suddenly got a wild hair up his ass, and had parked himself out front of Harrison's to wait for the right opportunity to plug the new sheriff of Clantick.

It hadn't come and it was probably just as well. It wasn't a job he should tackle alone. It was a job for two men, and since E. L. "Scratch" Lawson was now his only partner, it was a job for him and Scratch.

"You goddamn scaredy-cat," Bob mumbled to himself as he crossed an empty lot, angling southwest, toward the outskirts of Clantick, staring at the chalky puffs of dust kicked up by his boots. Afraid someone in town might recognize his horse from the train holdup, he'd left the line-back dun with Scratch and Evelyn at the abandoned shack they'd appropriated when they'd moved into town.

The shack sat in a ravine, below the wood-and-sod shanties that sat willy-nilly at the edge of town, flanked by privies, small barns, clotheslines, chicken coops, and trash piles. The air around there always smelled like burning trash and chicken shit. Near the shack in the ravine, a windmill had collapsed, taking out part of a corral.

The shack was an unpainted, thrown-together affair with a shake roof. Several of the shakes had blown off and been replaced by coffee tins hammered flat and by slats from packing crates. The place was apparently a stillborn ranch operation. Whoever had built it was long gone. From the trash inside the shack, Bob could tell it had been used by grubliners and other overnighters for the past several years. The small pile of wood outside the front door had most likely been stolen from the shacks up the butte.

The horses in the corral nickered as Bob jogged, half-sliding with his arms out for balance, down the slope and crossed the yard to the shack's door. He was about to turn the knob when he froze suddenly, and listened. From inside the shack he heard a staccato thumping, a girl sighing, and a man groaning.

Shaking his head and scowling, Bob pushed the door open. On one of the two lower bunks, Evelyn and Scratch were making love, Evelyn straddling Scratch and bouncing up and down as though riding a runaway ranch wagon. Scratch's big hands kneaded her hips as he tipped his head back, mouth open, and groaned like some wounded animal.

"Goddamnit, Evelyn," Bob yelled, fatigued from this disappointing start of the day, "I told you no fucking Scratch. Scratch, goddamnit, I told you—I don't want you fuckin' Evelyn!"

He took three quick steps, grabbed Evelyn by the arm, and yanked her off of Scratch. She screamed softly and fell to the floor. "Oh! Damn you, Bob!"

"Come on, Bob, we ain't done!" Scratch echoed, befuddled outrage bunching his unshaven cheeks.

"You ain't never gonna be done!" Bob yelled. "Now get yourself up and get dressed. We got work to do today."

Scratch rolled his head and slapped the grass-filled

mattress, looking pained. "Ah, goddamnit, anyway, Bob." He got up with his swollen penis sticking straight out of his faded red long johns, and ran outside.

When he was gone, Bob sat down at the small wood table. There was a bottle and three tin coffee cups on the table, and cigarette ashes and butts. There were also the leavings of the squirrel that had gotten in here during the night to clean up the corn bread leftover from last night's supper, and which all three people had been too drunk and sleepy to chase out.

Bob gave a sigh, poured some whiskey into a cup, and tossed it back.

"What'd you have to do that for, Uncle Bob?" Evelyn said, sitting naked on the floor and inspecting her knee. "I cut my knee on a nail."

"That's just tough," Bob said, not looking at her. "I told you I didn't want you diddling Scratch, didn't I?"

"But you know how Scratch is. He's too shy to ask for any lovin' from the girls uptown. He gets lonely layin' around listenin' to you and me."

"So you decided that since ol' Bob was gone, you'd just give Scratch a little lovin', that it?" He scowled at her, raising his lips like an angry dog. "You sure as hell never did that for me when you was diddlin' my little brother."

"That was different, Uncle Bob. Howie and me"— Evelyn's voice grew small and frail as a little girl's— "we was gonna be *married*."

Bob laughed brutally. "You think Howie was really gonna marry the likes of you? Ha! He was just diddlin' you till he tired of it. Then he was gonna send you back to the cheap little whorehouse you came from."

Evelyn looked at him wide-eyed, as though she were trying hard to keep a tight rein on her anger. "Don't you say that, Uncle Bob. Howie and me was gonna be married. We was gonna get out of here with the money from the train and live like decent folks."

"Like decent folks, eh?" Bob scoffed, pouring more whiskey into his cup. "Ha!" He tossed back the whiskey in a single gulp. "In the month we were up here livin' with Pa, Howie's diddled pret' near every whore on the Hi-Line. Ha!"

Evelyn stared at him, her chafed, naked breasts rising as she breathed. Her eyes smoldered like the coals under a burned-out fire. "That ain't true, Bob."

"Ha!" Bob said, splashing more whiskey in his cup.

"You take that back, Bob."

Bob tossed back the whiskey and laughed, spraying half the whiskey across the table. He snickered and wiped his mouth with his sleeve. At last he was having fun. He wasn't thinking about how scared he'd felt when he'd seen Stillman step out of that jailhouse.

Suddenly he realized Evelyn had gotten to her feet and was standing before him, fists balled at her sides.

Bob looked at her, a grinning sneer twisting his mouth. He sat there casually, insolently, right hand holding the cup. "There was one in partic'lar—I think her name was Candy; Howie called her 'Candy Ass'—she was givin' it to him for free there at the end. I think he was groomin' her to replace you." Bob chuckled and shook his head, as though recalling a fond moment from boyhood.

"Goddamn you, Bob!" Evelyn screamed.

Fists flying, she punched him about the head and

shoulders, shrieking something unintelligible. Bob laughed and covered his head with his upraised arms. Now and then she landed a punch on his cheek and forehead but there wasn't enough force behind the blows to do any real damage.

It didn't seem as though she were going to quit anytime soon, though, so Bob struggled to his feet, worked his arms out from his head, and wrestled Evelyn's arms down to her sides. She screamed and cursed and struggled against him, rolling her voluptuous naked body against his, arousing him.

Bob maneuvered his left hand around to the back of her neck and his right to her face, holding her firmly, and kissed her parted lips. It was like tossing kerosene on a fire. She renewed her violence so that Bob had to subdue her with two hard slaps across the mouth.

She slumped in his arms. He held her, guiding her across the room and onto the bunk where she and Scratch had been going at it five minutes before.

She lay there on her back, squirming and crying and covering her face with her arms. Watching her, his eyes smoldering with both hatred and lust, Bob unbuckled his cartridge belt and tossed his gun and holster on a chair.

Behind him, the door opened. Bob turned. It was Scratch looking sheepish and puzzled in his long johns. Bob flung an arm at him, index finger extended. "Out!"

Scratch quickly shut the door.

Bob turned back to Evelyn squirming around on the bunk. Watching her, he got more and more inflamed. In a minute, his clothes lay in piles on the floor. Bob bent down and worked his way between Evelyn's squirming legs, fighting her arms down at her sides. Getting one pinned under his knee, the other under his left hand, he hit her again—hard—with his right fist.

That took the air out of her sails.

After that, she just lay there staring at the top bunk while Uncle Bob rode her home.

17

Stillman walked into the rank darkness of Auld's Livery and asked for a horse. "I'll have to rent one until I have time to pick one out for buying," he told the surly liveryman, who was screwing a new plank lid on his oat bin.

"No need—you already have one," Auld said, customarily grouchy.

"Say again?"

"That young fella brought one into town for you a few days ago. He's out yonder." With his hammer, Auld indicated the corral back of the barn.

"What are you talking about, Auld?"

The big, gloomy man sighed, impatient. His voice rose as though trying to impart simple information to a half-wit. "Jody Harmon brought you a horse in a few days ago. Said it was a surprise and I wasn't s'posed to tell you till you come askin' for a ridin' horse. Well, now you come askin' for a ridin' horse, so I'm tellin' ya—he's out yonder. Saddle's in the tack room. You can saddle him yourself—I'm busy here and my boy just quit."

Frowning and thoughtfully puffing his cigar, Stillman walked down the alley and into the corral, where six or seven horses stood in the warming sun. A bay with a black mane was drinking from the scummy water trough. It was one of the finest horses Stillman had ever seen.

The horse turned to him, water dripping from its mouth. Stillman felt light-headed. He grinned and shook his head, recognizing the mount.

"Sweets."

The gelding had been Bill Harmon's favorite horse. Jody had turned its reins over to Stillman while he'd broken up Donovan Hobbs's rustling operation two years ago. Now apparently, he was turning it over to him again—permanently.

He walked slowly over to the horse, ran his hand down its neck, scratched under its chin, and spoke softly, letting Sweets get used to the sound of his voice again.

Stillman found Bill Harmon's old saddle in the tack room. He secured it to Sweets after bridling the horse, and slid his Henry into the boot strapped to the saddle. "Just like old times, eh, Sweets?" he said, mounting.

He rode the horse into the barn and down the alley, stopping behind Auld, now sipping coffee on his new oat bin lid. "What do I owe you for stabling and feed?"

"Nothin'," Auld said dully. "Harmon talked the city council into springing for it. Don't ask me why. I never get nothin' handed to me."

"What's the occasion, Auld?"

"Huh?"

"You're downright cheery this morning," Stillman said dryly.

He touched his spurs to Sweets's flanks and left the barn, hitting the street at a trot. He clomped across the wooden bridge over the Milk River and headed north on the Medicine Hat freight road, twin wagon ruts snaking up the river bluffs and out across the undulating prairie, bright in the mid-morning sun.

The relatively featureless terrain was interrupted here and there by wooded watercourses, small ranch operations, and farms with patches of oats and hay flanking a sod shack and pole corral, two or three hard-eyed youngsters staring as Stillman cantered past, ignoring his wave.

At a shack nestled in a creek hollow, a short-haired mongrel came out to bark and nip at Sweets. It turned around in a cloud of dust and, satisfied it had done its duty, headed back to the shack's sagging porch, where an old, bearded man in coveralls sat smoking a corncob pipe and a girl no more than ten knelt beside a butter churn. They, too, did not return Stillman's wave.

That the Hi-Line remained a hard land, only recently settled, was evident in their cold, wary eyes.

Judson's Store was little more than a log shack with a crude sign over the front door. It stank of beer and whiskey fermenting in cedar barrels in the long, dry grass out back, where a privy sat sunbaked and leaning toward the hillock that flanked it. There was a two-wheeled cart out front, a gray-muzzled mule in the traces. Three children and a young woman sat on the steps. Stillman was surprised when they returned his wave. Newcomers.

He followed the trail westward, where a wide, shallow valley opened, creased in its center by a two-wheeled wagon track littered with all ages of horse dung and fresh shoe tracks. The sun was heating up, scorching the weeds and filling the air with the smell of dry sage. Gophers scuttled in the grass, and hawks hunted the low, barren ridge on Stillman's left. Here and there a choke-cherry bush hunkered along a hillock, the bitter berries still green as peas.

Stillman saw someone on the left ridge out of the corner of his eye. He turned his head to see a rider silhouetted against the sky. The man held a carbine in his hands, its butt on his hip. Swinging his gaze to the other ridge, Stillman saw another man positioned much like the first, a carbine prominently displayed.

Stillman let Sweets continue walking, holding the horse's reins loosely in his hands, fighting the urge to release the hammer thong over his .44. He knew these men were Norman Billingsley's gunslicks—he'd been expecting them. What he did not know is what they were going to do.

He supposed he was crazy, riding out here alone, but he'd sent a message with the two men who'd attacked him in Sam Wah's, and you either followed through with a threat or tossed your badge in a drawer.

Suddenly a gun barked. Stillman heard the eery whine of the bullet just before it passed over his head, snagging his hat. He turned to see the Stetson lying in the grass, levitating on the breeze, about to turn over and roll. Someone laughed, and he turned to the ridge on his left, where the rider there, silhouetted against the sky, lifted his head, chuckling.

When the breeze died, he heard a "Hee-hee," from the rider on the ridge to his right.

"You don't want to come no closer, or you're gonna lose more than your hat," the man on the right ridge said.

"I'm here to see Norman Billingsley," Stillman called.

The man shook his head. "Mr. Billingsley's busy today."

Stillman spurred Sweets forward. "I left word with my deputy where I'm going. I don't come back later this afternoon, he has orders to send for federal marshals down in Helena."

"Hear that, Chuck?" the man on the right ridge said. "He's sent for federal marshals."

"I heard," Chuck said.

"That shakes my boots off, it does," the other man said. He lifted his carbine and fired. The round barked off a stone three feet in front of Sweets, who stopped suddenly, agitated, and crow-hopped. Stillman held tight to the reins, setting his jaw in anger.

"Why don't you two chickenshits come down here and face me like men?"

The man on the right ridge spurred down off the slope, coming at a lazy pace, slouching in his saddle with casual insolence. On the left ridge, the man called Chuck followed suit. Stillman held the nervous Sweets still and watched the men approach. The horse blew and toothed its bit. Muscles rippled in its neck.

The men stopped their horses about ten yards on either side of Stillman. They were hard, pathological-looking men in filthy cream dusters, with fishy eyes. They held their carbines on their hips; both smiled. Holsters were tied just above their right knees.

"There, now isn't that better?" Stillman asked them, turning his head to regard them both. "It's hard to converse when you have to yell."

"I got nothin' to say to you," Chuck said. He had large, deep-set eyes and the sallow face of a lunger.

The other man said, "We got orders to stop anyone coming to see Mr. Billingsley—especially the dumb sumbitch who gave two of his men a hard time in Sam Wah's yesterday." The man smiled, narrowing his eyes. "You got balls, comin' out here. Don't you know you're gonna die?"

"We all have to die someday," Stillman said with a shrug.

He didn't want to take his eyes off these two to make sure, but he was certain more men were approaching from ahead. He sensed these two knew it, and were waiting for them. From the smugly cunning expressions on their faces they no doubt had orders to string Stillman from the nearest tree.

Billingsley had nerve—Stillman gave him that. And a total disregard for the law, which told the lawman the man had to be backed by someone in town. Someone with power.

Stillman met Chuck's fishy eyes and returned the man's grin. He could tell from that grin these men indeed planned to kill him. Figuring he had to act before the other riders got there, he reached for his .44. In half a second, the gun was in his hand, catching the two men on either side of him completely off guard. They'd fully expected themselves to make the first move, when the others arrived.

The revolver came up and barked. Two shots. Both men went off the backs of their horses with only Chuck giving a yell. They were dead before they hit the ground, hats rolling over the weeds, dusters flapping on the wind.

Stillman jerked a look down the trail. The other men—there were seven or eight, it appeared—were galloping toward him now, and spreading out. In a split second, Stillman knew what he was going to do. He reined Sweets around and spurred him back in the direction he'd come, feeling semi-naked without his hat.

When about a hundred yards separated him from the other men, who were firing at him with pistols, Stillman swung off the trail and headed across the prairie, watching for gopher holes. All he needed was for Sweets to go down with a broken leg. It would mean death for them both.

When Sweets had pounded over a grassy rise, Stillman suddenly brought the horse to a halt and slipped out of the leather, shucking his Henry rifle in one quick motion. The well-trained bay standing ground-hitched behind him, Stillman ran up the rise, fell to his hands and knees, and crawled to the lip. Jacking a shell in the chamber, he peered across the prairie, at the eight riders closing on him fast.

Heart pumping, the old excitement flowing, he took aim at one of the galloping riders, about fifty yards away from him now, and fired. The man's horse suddenly lunged sideways as the wounded rider toppled from his saddle. Both his feet caught in the stirrups and he hung down one side of his horse, whipped like a rag doll, before his right boot finally freed itself. Then he plunged and was dragged for several feet, until the left boot worked free, as well.

It took the other riders several seconds to realize they were being fired upon. In the meantime, another of Stillman's rounds plunged into a chest, tore through a heart, and split a backbone, laying the rider out flat against his cantle and bedroll. The man was dead as the bucking horse tossed him from the saddle like so much human compost, then trampled him, rolling him under its hooves for several yards before the man lay inert, impossibly twisted, in a sage clump.

Stillman stared down the Henry's barrel, trying to pick out another target as the riders dismounted their screaming, plunging horses, and scrambled for cover. The problem was there wasn't much. All they could do was run for a hollow in the deep grass and hope they didn't buy a bullet along the way.

The horses kicking up dust, it was hard to find a target in the screaming, yelling, cursing melee of horses and men, but Stillman did. Retreating toward the hollow, one man straightened suddenly with the hot pain of the bullet that had torn into his left buttock and lodged in his hip. Stillman hadn't aimed for the man's ass, but through the dust and horses it was hard to find a target. It didn't matter. The man was out of commission—probably for the rest of his miserable life.

Rifles popped as the riders, having taken cover in two shallow depressions about fifty and seventy yards away, returned fire. The lead thumped into the grass around Stillman, spraying him with dust and sod.

Lowering his Henry, he turned and ran crouching into the hollow behind him, where Sweets stood looking agitated, swinging his tail. Stillman shoved the rifle in its boot and mounted the bay, spurring off down a shallow, bending crease in the prairie, keeping his head low as the riders' lead whined through the air above him.

After galloping several yards, the crease turned back in the direction of the riders. Stillman brought the bay up the other side and headed across the prairie in the general direction of Clantick.

The rifle fire died away behind him as he left Billingsley's hammerheads in his dust. He kept moving just the same, knowing that when the riders had discovered he'd fled, they'd follow. You didn't kill or maim three of their kind and not have them running you down like a swarm of angry hornets.

As he rode, he quickly figured his odds had grown better in the past several minutes. There had been a total of ten men after him—probably most of Billingsley's entire roll. Stillman had managed to kill or seriously wound five. That meant only five remained.

He knew he should go back to Clantick and gather Leon and a posse before heading back to the Billingsley place. But he wasn't sure he'd be able to gather enough men willing to ride against Norman Billingsley's hired guns. Besides, the five behind him could very well ride him down before he got to town.

No, he was too deep in the game to toss in the pasteboards now. After quick deliberation, he decided his best chance at getting Billingsley was making the five remaining riders believe he was heading back to Clantick. That shouldn't be hard. They'd be expecting as much. What they wouldn't be expecting was for him to do just what he intended—swinging around and heading back toward the Billingsley place and facing old Norman himself, arresting the crooked rancher and taking him back to town.

He'd worry about Judge Humperdink and Bernard McFadden later. There were enough men against Billingsley on the city council to increase the possibility of a fair trial—in the court of a judge from another county—and to get the man convicted of harboring fugitives and conspiring to commit murder.

Stillman headed straight out across the open prairie, spurring Sweets well ahead of the five riders who had remounted and were again behind him. When he came to a creek sheathed by tall grass and willows, he went on across, splashing through the mud and scaring up a couple mud hens and a Canada goose. He found a trail of bent weeds where a deer had recently passed, and followed it for about a hundred yards toward town.

Then he swung Sweets sharply west, around a butte with a shelving clay bank. The grass here was medium height and thick, and unless the riders suspected his ruse, they'd give little thought to watching for his tracks. Deer in all directions had made plenty of confusing signs. Billingsley's men would think he'd headed for Clantick.

He rode east for half a mile, then swung back north. He came to a low rimrock, dismounted, and climbed to the ridge with his field glasses. Lying just beneath the crest of the ridge, he brought the glasses to his eyes and trained them south, around where he'd swung eastward after leaving the creek.

After a minute he smiled. Sure enough, Billingsley's riders had taken the bait, and were headed straight south of the creek, in the general direction of Clantick. From this distance they were little more than five brown dots riding singly and abreast, loping their horses through the short grass and sage, climbing a low rise toward the Milk River buttes beyond.

Sighing with relief, Stillman returned to Sweets, stowed the glasses in his saddlebags, and headed north, following shallow watercourses back to the valley where he'd first been attacked. He followed the valley for another mile, until he spied a big, unfinished house sitting on a bluff rising majestically above the prairie. The house, only two-thirds built, was a beaut, with four dormers, a gargantuan stone chimney, and a wraparound porch.

Stillman tapped the butt of his .44 compulsively, making sure it was there. "Come on, Sweets," he said as he spurred the horse toward the house. "Let's see if anybody's home."

18

Stillman tethered Sweets in the scrub oaks and cedars below the house, shucked his rifle, and climbed the butte. He hunkered down on his haunches staring at the big porch from the weeds, the house looming before him bright in the westering light.

There were no sounds or horses to indicate that anyone was in the house. Nevertheless, he ran in a half-crouch to the big structure smelling of pine resin, mounted the porch, knelt, and looked around listening. There was no glass in any of the windows, so if someone were inside, he'd have heard them. Unless they'd seen him and were staying put.

He sensed no one was here, but just to make sure he entered the house through a doorless frame, and walked through every room in the cavernous dwelling. So far it had been furnished only with sawhorses, makeshift benches, odds and ends of saws and other woodworking tools, and all shapes and sizes of planed lumber stamped by a mill in Great Falls.

Satisfied he was alone in the house, Stillman stole a look out a door on the opposite side and gazed down the bluff to where a temporary headquarters had been set up on an open flat of grassless ground packed hard by horses and cattle. There was a low-roofed, log house chinked with adobe. Across from it sat a long bunkhouse and a pole barn with an anvil and a blacksmith's forge abutting the near end.

Near a windmill and corral, a tarpaulin had been erected on cottonwood poles. Beneath the tarpaulin stood a short, stocky man in a flat-brimmed Stetson, dress slacks, and a waistcoat. He crouched over a small table at which he worked with a knife, the knife blade winking in the sun slanting through the poles. Behind the man, two other men perched on the top corral slat, rifles across their knees. Bodyguards, no doubt. Billingsley had got wind that Stillman was after him.

Stillman ducked back inside the house, turned, and headed for the other side. He stepped off the opposite porch, descended the butte about twenty yards, from where he wouldn't be seen by the three men below the house, and jogged north. When he'd brought the barn between him and the men, he ran to it, stepped inside, walking quietly so as not to frighten the saddle stock stabled there, and crept down the alley to where the opposite doors opened onto the ranch yard.

Reaching the doors, he stepped behind the wall and stole a look outside. About thirty feet away were the two men perched on the corral and the third man, an older man, working under the tarpaulin. They were facing the big house, only their profiles visible to Stillman.

He knew instinctively that the older, gray-haired gent, thick through the hips, arms, and shoulders, was Billingsley. Old Norman himself, gutting and scaling a fish—one of many, it appeared, from the bucket of bloody water at his feet.

"There, look at that," he said, holding up a hefty carp to the two men behind him. "That's the biggest one yet!"

He laughed loudly and dropped the fish in another pail. Then he reached into a canvas sack hanging from one of the poles over which the tarpaulin was draped, and produced another carp he must have snagged in the Milk River, or one of the creeks that drained into it. Stillman could smell the rank, muddy odor of the bottom prowlers from here.

"Yes, sir, Mr. Billingsley," one of the men said ingratiatingly, but without fervor, "you sure can catch the carp."

"My grandfather used to snag these suckers in the Brazos—wagon loads of 'em—and smoke them up for supper. You say neither of you boys has ever eaten carp?"

"Can't say as I have, Mr. Billingsley."

"Well, you're in for a real treat, then. Yessir, a real treat!" The old man laughed as he picked up the wood-handled scaler and went to work on the carp, the tail of which he held with a pliers. The scales flew around the table like fine hail. The cowboys on the corral looked on with reticent expressions on their faces.

Stillman thumbed back the Henry's hammer to full cock, bringing the rifle to his shoulder. He yelled, "You two drop those irons, or I'm gonna blow you off that corral like a couple target cans!"

Both men jerked around at Stillman, lifting their rifles.

"Drop 'em!" Stillman urged.

One dropped off the corral and brought his rifle to bear. Stillman plugged him through the shoulder, twisting him around and throwing him over the middle corral slat, where he hung screaming like a diamondback on a stick.

The other sat his perch, jerking his rifle chest high and squeezing off a thunderous round. The slug thumped into the wall about two feet to Stillman's left. It continued through the wall and twanged into a tin bucket, the sharp ping setting the stable horses to nickering and thumping around in their stalls.

Before the man on the corral could jack another shell, Stillman pinked him through the right cheek, dropping him backward off the corral. He landed on the top of his head, snapping his neck. He was on his hands and knees, forehead pressed to the ground, as though in the midst of some Middle Eastern prayer; his boots digging into the ground for several seconds, as if attempting to run. Then he fell sideways and lay idle.

The first man Stillman had shot had managed to climb over the middle corral slat, losing his rifle in the process. Raging, blood running down his shoulder, he drew his sidearm and fired twice before diving for cover behind a feed trough. Stillman fired three rounds through the trough. The man stood, his face and neck bloody, screamed something unintelligible, turned, fired into the air, turned again, and fell over the legs of his friend.

Stillman looked at the man under the tarpaulin. He was staring at Stillman sourly, frozen there with the fish scaler in his hand. He held the other hand halfway to his chest, the bloody, sausage-like fingers curled crablike.

"You armed?" Stillman asked him as he approached, the Henry held out from his waist, and glanced around cautiously.

"Nope."

"You Billingsley?"

"Who wants to know?"

"Ben Stillman."

Billingsley's wary eyes drifted to the two dead men in his corral. "You're kind of off your feed today, aren't ya?"

"I told them to drop their weapons. That's what happens when you don't listen to your elders. Drop that scaler and step back from the table. I'm gonna search you."

"I told you, I'm not carrying a weapon. That's what they were for."

"Just the same . . ." Holding his rifle waist high, Stillman patted the man down, turned him brusquely around, and patted him down again. "You don't look like the type to carry a hideaway in your shoe, but if you are, you best produce it now or plan on eating it later."

Billingsley's shock and surprise had turned to rage. "What the hell is this about?"

"You're under arrest."

"For what?"

"Harboring fugitives and conspiring to commit murder."

"You're joking!"

"Do I look like it?"

The man's fleshy face, with its small blue eyes slanting devilishly, turned even redder than before. He stared at Stillman, incensed, at a loss for words. He looked as though he might explode. Stillman grabbed him by the shoulder and gave him a tug toward the barn. "Go saddle a horse. You're coming with me."

"You fool," the man blubbered, voice quivering. "You can't do this to me. By god, I've got an interest in the

bank and half a dozen stores on First Street! Without
me, that town wouldn't be a town! You can't arrest me
for . . . for . . . one man's indiscretion." His voice had
lost some of its anger and had acquired a helpless urging.

"You broke the law. I don't care who you are or what
you've done. You're going to jail. You and Rafe Paul—
if he's still alive, that is."

"What do you mean 'if he's still alive'?" The man
stopped at the barn entrance and turned to Stillman un-
easily.

"I shot up about five of your men on my way in here.
The rest are following my trail toward Clantick—or so
they think."

The man's eyes narrowed as they took a piqued appraisal of the legendary lawman. "You really are Stillman, aren't you? I thought they were just jawing about
getting you here."

"In the flesh."

"I thought you were dead."

Stillman sighed. He gestured into the musty, ammo-
niac darkness of the barn's interior with his rifle barrel,
wanting to get moving. You never knew when a few of
Billingsley's remaining riders were going to get savvy
and double back.

Billingsley ignored the gesture. The anger had left his
face, giving him a deflated look, the big face with its
deep lines around the eyes and mouth sagging toward
his chin. "Let's be reasonable, Stillman. Let's talk re-
alistically. Do you really think Judge Humperdink is going to convict me of any of the things you're accusing
me of?"

"That's not my concern," Stillman said. "But I'll tell you this—if your men would have let me ride out here unharassed, and if you would have let me take Rafe Paul into custody, things would have looked a might prettier for you. I might not have taken you in. But now you're an accessory to assaulting a peace officer in addition to resisting arrest."

He paused thoughtfully before continuing. "But then there's also the little problem of Ralph Merchant, who was lynched north of town not long after being seen with McFadden." Stillman shook his head. "All that, in addition to harboring fugitives . . ."

"I had nothing to do with Merchant's hanging," the rancher snapped, anger returning to flush the big knobs of his cheeks. "That was McFadden's doing. He killed the previous sheriff, as well."

Stillman frowned and cocked his head. "Why . . . ?"

"Because of his wife."

Stillman's frown became a wince. "His wife?"

Billingsley turned away sharply, as though catching himself. He looked around the barn as if searching for something. "Listen, Stillman. I . . . I've got a deal for you."

"Tell me about McFadden's wife." Stillman was thinking of Fay, a pinprick of apprehension crowhopping along his spine.

"How about I give you five thousand dollars? Will you get out of town?"

"I want to hear about McFadden's wife."

"What are you making? Seventy-five, a hundred dollars a month? I heard your wife is used to a little more than that." A sneer puckered the fleshy man's lips.

Stillman grabbed him by his collar and brought his face up to the man's forehead, looking down into the rancher's beady little washed-out eyes. Carp scales salted his brow. "Goddamn you, tell me about Mc-Fadden's wife!"

There was real fear in the man's face now, as he returned Stillman's stare with a hesitant one of his own. "I . . . I can't say any more. I've said enough the way it is. Bernard and I . . . we're partners, for chrissakes. He watches out for my interests, and I watch out for his."

Stillman twisted the man's collar, lifting him onto his toes. Billingsley took several jerky sidesteps trying to regain his balance, his breath coming short and raspy. His face turned redder, but he offered nothing more than a quick shake of his head.

"Go ahead and arrest me. But you'll learn nothing more about McFadden's wife. You might as well take the money I've offered you and get the hell out of town. You might have been a hell of a lawman in your prime, but even back then you couldn't have handled the situation you're in now." In spite of the windpipe Stillman had pinched half-shut by twisting the man's collar, Billingsley stretched a thin smile.

Stillman scowled at the man's face, their heads less than six inches apart. Stillman gave him a heave. Billingsley went stumbling backward, making little grunts of protest as he lost his footing and fell on his ass. His eyes stayed with Stillman. The half-smile returned to his lips.

Stillman set down the rifle and began rolling up his shirtsleeves. "I've never bullied information out of a prisoner before," he said tightly. "There's a first time for everything. You can tell me now what you meant about McFadden killing Merchant because of his wife, or you can tell me in about five minutes, around a mouthful of broken teeth . . ."

Halfway to the rancher, watching him now with true trepidation, Stillman stopped. He'd heard something. Pounding hooves. Grabbing his rifle, he ran to the barn doors and looked out.

He cursed.

Five riders were pounding down from the big house on sweat-foamed horses.

19

The blaze-faced black pounded down the trail toward Clantick.

The beat of its hooves rose on the quiet afternoon air and merged with the scraping of crickets and cooing of meadowlarks, kicking up dust and throwing it behind on the sun-scorched grass.

Fay hunkered low in the saddle, urging the animal with her heels. She didn't hear the crickets or the birds. She didn't hear the pounding of the horse's hooves along the hard-packed trail. She didn't see her hair bouncing in her eyes or feel it blowing behind her in the wind.

"Iris, stop!" was all she heard—her own voice—over and over again. Then she heard the crack of the pistol, saw the hole open in Iris McFadden's head . . . saw the blood. . . .

"Oh, god—what have I done?" she mumbled, her lips quivering, her expression at once horrified and sad.

Iris McFadden, whatever she'd been, was dead because of her.

"Oh, god—what have I *done*!"

She brushed the tears from her cheeks with her hand and hunkered low in the saddle as the stallion pounded northward. She wanted only one thing now and that was to see Ben and tell him what had happened, that she'd had to kill Iris McFadden, that it had been Iris who had bushwhacked him yesterday and that her brother Bernard had arranged Ralph Merchant's murder.

Because of the women . . . all those poor, murdered women. . . .

Then she wanted Ben to wrap his arms around her and hold her like a child while she cried.

Then she wanted him to take her away from here. A long, long ways away. . . . This was no place for her and Ben. She should have known that, after her miserable experience here with Donovan Hobbs.

When she reached the outskirts of Clantick, the sun was angling low in the west. It had to be at least three in the afternoon, she realized, as though suddenly stirring from a dream. She reined the horse to a canter only when she reached First Street, where people along the boardwalks stopped to regard her wistfully. She imagined she made quite a sight—the new sheriff's wife storming into town on a sweat-matted horse belonging to the town banker. Her clothes were dusty and her hair was disheveled, but she made no attempt to compose herself.

Reining the black to a halt at the hitch rail before the jail, she climbed down from the saddle, tied the horse, flung open the door, and ran into Ben's office. Her nose was immediately assaulted by thick wood smoke hanging in the air like lace canopies. It stung her eyes and made her lungs clench.

"Whoa now," came a man's startled voice accompanied by the squawk of a chair. "I don't think the new sheriff would feel too kindly about having his door torn off its hinges, even by someone pretty as you."

Fay stared at the stocky, red-haired, red-whiskered

gent in Ben's chair. There was a bottle before him on the desk, and a tin cup. He was sitting as though he'd just removed his feet from the desktop, and was regarding Fay with patronizing humor. This stranger in Ben's office, coupled with the smoke hanging in the air like gauze, intensified Fay's confusion. She was at a loss for words.

"Sorry about the smoke," the stranger said, waving his arm and wincing. "In the process of boiling coffee, I discovered the flue is plugged." He coughed and regarded the black stove in the center of the room.

"Who are you?" Fay managed, still standing where she'd stopped before the open door.

"Clyde Evans. Doctor and coroner. The sheriff's not in." The man's eyes traveled down Fay's body, a smile etched on his lips. "Maybe I can help."

"Where's Ben?"

"Said he was heading up north to the Billingsley ranch. I expected him back by now—if he was *coming* back, that is." The man's face suddenly fell as a thought occurred to him. "Oh, shit. You're the missus, aren't you?"

Fay hadn't heard the question. Her heart was pounding, her mind racing. If Ben had gone to the Billingsley ranch and had not yet returned, he could very well be in trouble. It may not have been Billingsley who'd ordered Ralph Merchant killed, but it had been his men who had done the killing—on orders from Bernard McFadden. Who's to say McFadden hadn't ordered them to kill Ben?

"Oh, god," Fay said, slumping against the wall. She felt faint and weak with fear and shock over what had happened . . . over what was happening. What if Ben was dead? She suddenly felt more dark and lonely and afraid than she'd ever felt in her life.

Oh, why had they come here?

"Whoa there!" Evans said, jumping out of his chair and bounding to Fay's side. He grabbed her arms to keep her from falling. "Easy now, easy. Here—let's get you in the chair over here before you fall and hurt yourself. I'm sorry about what I said. I didn't realize . . . well, I didn't realize you were Stillman's wife. . . ."

He led her to the chair behind the desk. As they got to it, Fay took a deep breath and composed herself, fighting off the weakness and nausea that had accompanied the horrible possibility of Ben's death. She pushed away from Evans, swallowing, swiping her hair from her eyes.

With controlled fervor, she said, "I . . . have to find Ben."

Evans shook his head. "Well, like I said—"

"Where's Leon?"

"The deputy? On the way over here I saw him in the alley behind the flophouses, breaking up a fight."

"Show me," Fay urged.

Evans's eyes, glazed with drink, were perplexed. He shrugged. "All right—come along," he said, removing his battered derby from the desk and snugging it over his thick red hair. He picked up the cigar smoldering in an ashtray, stuck it in his mouth, and headed out the door.

Fay followed him west along the boardwalk. Turning a corner and starting down a side street, they saw Leon walking toward them with a hatless, staggering man in tow. Leon was lecturing the man.

"Now every time you boys come to town and get in a disagreement over the girls, you're gonna have three days in the lockup. Understand?"

"It was a *friendly* disagreement," the man whined.

Leon shook his head. "Where I come from, we don't call fightin' with broken whiskey bottles friendly."

"But, I'm tellin' ya—it weren't me that started it!"

"And I'm tellin' you—" Leon looked up and saw Evans and Fay. He frowned. "Mrs. Stillman . . . what—?"

Fay ran to him and grabbed his arm, ignoring the drunk beside him, in spite of the man's putrid stench of busthead. "Leon, we have to find Ben."

"What's wrong, Fay?"

"I . . . I killed Mrs. McFadden." Tears welled in Fay's eyes. She sobbed.

Leon looked at her uncomprehendingly. "What are you talking about?"

Fay's thoughts were scattered. With both hands she squeezed Leon's left arm, trying to maintain control of herself and implore Leon at the same time. "We have to find Ben. Bernard McFadden killed—had someone kill—Ralph Merchant. Iris was the one who ambushed Ben—"

"Wait a minute, wait a minute, wait a minute," Leon implored, holding out his hand. He turned to the drunk. "All right, Buzz, you got lucky today. I'm suspending your sentence as long as you go right on back to your farm and stay away from town for a month. Understand?"

The drunk farmer blinked at him. "You mean it, dep'ty?"

"Git! Scram!" Leon yelled, and watched the man in coveralls turn and move drunkenly across the street, toward the feed barn.

Before making the opposite boardwalk, the man glanced over his shoulder at Leon several times, nearly getting hit by an Indian family in a buckboard. Before the harness shop, he stopped, turned to Leon, and grinned a toothless grin.

"You go home now!" Leon ordered him, jabbing a paternal finger at the end of his upraised arm.

The man waved and ambled off toward the barn. Leon turned to Fay, taking her by the arm and leading her up the boardwalk. "Let's go back to the office, and you tell me everything from the beginning. Slow and clear so I can understand it."

Stillman shoved Billingsley toward the barn doors. "To the cabin—*move!*"

The rancher had heard the horses and knew his men were returning. He grinned at Stillman and stood stiffly within the barn's shadows. "I'm not going anywhere."

Stillman turned to him and struck the butt of his rifle against the man's temple. Billingsley yelled and stumbled backward, clutching his head. Stillman grabbed him and shoved him again toward the cabin. The man cooperated halfheartedly, knowing if he didn't another head-clubbing was imminent.

Stillman ran pushing Billingsley ahead of him. At the cabin door, he turned. The five cowboys had seen him and were yelling back and forth, spurring their galloping mounts toward him. Stillman knelt, brought the rifle to his shoulder, and snapped off five quick shots. He only grazed one of the riders, but it was enough to slow them all down and make them think twice about storming the cabin.

Stillman turned to the open door, where Billingsley stood holding a handkerchief to his bleeding temple and looking beyond Stillman at the riders who were dismounting and scrambling for cover. He gave Stillman another wry smile.

"It's all over, Stillman. You're a dead man if you don't let me go."

Stillman pushed the man into the cabin, nearly knocking him off his feet. Then the lawman closed the door and brought the plank down over it, snugging the two-by-six into the steel U-straps on either side of the jamb. Turning, he saw there were three sashed windows in the cramped, three-room structure. He ran to them and quickly drew the roll shades closed.

"What's the point, Stillman?" Billingsley barked. "There's five men out there! You're surrounded!"

Stillman had just finished drawing the third shade closed when a bullet exploded the glass, spraying the sharp-edged shards across the kitchen table and plank countertops. Another slug barked through the door and into the opposite log wall.

"You better get down, or they're gonna kill us both," Stillman warned Billingsley.

Billingsley did as he was told, hunkering on his butt against the wall. He lifted his head toward a window and yelled, "Stop shooting, goddamnit! *I'm* in here. This is Billingsley. Hold your goddamn fire!"

It was Stillman's turn for a wry smile. "I don't think they care."

Billingsley muttered a curse as he glanced around to see out one of the windows without exposing himself to his hired predators, who might or might not shoot at anything that moved.

Stillman moved across the room, crouched beneath a window, and took up position between the window and the door. From here he could slide a look out the window in the direction from which the riders had come. One was hunkered in the corral, peering out from under the middle slat, not far from the two dead men. Another man's rifle and hat brim poked up from behind the water trough.

Stepping quickly past the window and pressing his back to the wall, he glanced out the window again, from the other side. From here he could see the barn. One man peered around the open doors at this end; two more stood in the shadows at the other end, staring this way.

Stillman sighed and looked for options. There weren't many. Since there was only one door to the cabin, there was no way he could make a run for it before being gunned down in the barnyard. He could try to pick off each of the five remaining riders, but that would only get him into a firefight, and he doubted he could kill them all before running out of ammo, even if Billingsley had more than the one rifle hanging on the wall behind the table, and two or three boxes of shells hid away somewhere.

No, fighting it out with these men wasn't the answer.

He cursed silently to himself, his mind racing in circles, trying to come up with a solution to the impossible dilemma in which he found himself. He could just sit here and hope that, in time, Leon would come looking for him. But there weren't too many hours of daylight left. Come dark, these men might just try to burn him out. He doubted Billingsley could control a rough-cut crew like this from within the cabin.

Unless he called them off now.

Stillman looked at the rancher. "Tell them to throw their rifles down. Tell them if they don't, I'm going to shoot you. I doubt there's any love lost between you and these hired guns, but they'd want you to stay around long enough to pay them off."

Billingsley laughed. "You won't shoot me."

"Oh?"

"You shoot me and there'll be nothing stopping those men from storming in here."

Stillman lifted the rifle to his shoulder and took careful aim at the rancher. Billingsley looked at him horrified. "What the hell—?"

"I didn't say I'd kill you. If you haven't called them all out in the open and told them to drop their guns, I'm going to blow your kneecap off."

"You wouldn't—"

Stillman clipped the rancher's sentence with a 260-grain slug from his Henry. The bullet creased the rancher's earlobe. His head jerked and his eyes grew wide with fear and outrage. He lifted his hand to his ear and inspected the blood on his finger.

"You goddamn savage!"

"Call them out here where I can see them!"

A voice rose from outside. "You okay, Mr. Billingsley?"

Billingsley turned to the window. "Throw down your

guns and come out here. If you don't, this madman is going to start filling me with lead."

"Then we'll fill *him* with lead," came a voice from the barn.

Billingsley's voice cracked as he shouted, "Get out here, goddamnit, and throw out your irons!"

There was a long silence. In the hot cabin, flies buzzed against the windows. Billingsley breathed noisily. Sweat had popped out on his forehead and dribbled down his face. His shirt and waistcoat stuck to him.

With the barrel of the Henry, Stillman broke the glass out of the window. "You got thirty more seconds," he called. "Then I start blowing your employer's kneecaps off. I have a feeling he won't feel much like paying you after that."

About five seconds later, the two men in the corral ducked through the slats and walked toward the cabin, staring warily at the window where Stillman stood. They held their rifles in one hand, barrels aimed at the ground. Stillman saw that one of the men wore a white bandage over his nose, and that his eyes were blue as ripe plums. It was the man he'd tossed through Sam Wah's window, and he didn't look any happier today than he had then.

When they were about fifty feet from the door, both men dropped their Winchesters. They turned their heads toward the barn, and Stillman did likewise. The three men from the barn were heading this way. One held his rifle out before him, ready for anything. The one in the middle held his carbine toward the ground, while the third held his over his shoulder, an insolent grin on his savage, unshaven face.

"Drop 'em," Stillman ordered them warningly, when they came up and stood with the others.

They dropped the rifles and stood there, waiting, scowling, glancing at each other.

"Now unfasten those cartridge belts and chuck them this way."

Slowly, grudgingly, they did as they were told.

Stillman turned to Billingsley. "Let's go," he said.

When the man had stood and moved toward him, Stillman got behind him and shoved him out the door. They walked up to the five men facing the cabin behind a nest of rifles and gunbelts. Shadows were drifting over the barnyard as the sun angled downward. The horses in the corral were staring this way. One blew and whinnied.

"You son of a bitch," the man with the broken nose growled. Stillman remembered his name was Claude.

"I reckon I have a volunteer," Stillman said brightly, smiling at the man.

"Huh?"

"Claude, I need a horse saddled and brought to me. You have five minutes. I see you come out of that barn with anything but a good saddle horse, I'm gonna blow you to kingdom come, and I'm gonna throw in one of your pals for good measure."

The man scowled, his face glowing red around the bandage.

"Run!" Stillman shouted.

Claude cursed, turned, and walked to the barn.

"Any of you boys happen to be Rafe Paul?" Stillman asked the remaining four men.

They looked at each other. "Nope," one of them said.

"You're an ornery son of a bitch," one of the other gunmen snarled.

"It's the job," Stillman returned.

"You won't get away with this," another said. "You'll never make it to town."

"If I see any of you behind me after I've ridden out of here, I'm gonna shoot ol' Norman. Tell 'em, Norm."

Billingsley glared at Stillman. Then he glanced at the four men gathered before him. "Stay put." He dropped his eyes and stood there, head bowed, like a whipped bully in a schoolyard.

The man on Stillman's far right focused on something around the cabin. His gaze held there, his face acquiring a peculiar expression. His eyes went to Stillman. Back in them a ways Stillman detected humor.

"You see something out there?" Stillman asked him.

The man bunched his lips and lifted his shoulders. "Not a thing."

Stillman knew the man had seen something. Either that or he wanted Stillman to believe something was there, so he'd turn and look, and leave himself open. That's all it would take, he figured, to have all four of these men swarming on him like yellow jackets.

"Hurry it up in there!" Stillman yelled to the barn, getting edgy.

The man who'd seen something grinned with his eyes.

Claude appeared leading a claybank horse out of the barn. As he approached the cabin, his eyes wandered left, focusing on something just over Stillman's right shoulder. The hair on the back of Stillman's neck pricked. The man with the broken nose stopped, looked at the lawman, and grinned.

"Hold it right there, you son of a fuckin' bitch!"

The voice—more of a low, grating rasp—came from behind Stillman. Stillman's heart thumped and his head grew hot. He tensed. Wet snakes wriggled up his back.

"Throw that rifle down," the man behind him said tightly, through gritted teeth.

Stillman looked at the men before him, and at Billingsley. They were all smiling as though they'd just seen a pretty girl walk past.

"Drop the rifle," Billingsley said through a grin, eyes twinkling with delight. "Then turn around and meet Rafe Paul."

20

Stillman off-cocked the Henry, grabbed the barrel, and lowered the butt to the ground. Billingsley moved forward and took the rifle out of his hands, chuckling.

Stillman turned. The man before him stood in a half crouch against the corner of the cabin. He was a short, wiry, muscular man with a narrow, hollow-cheeked face, a beak nose, a thin brown mustache, and a two-day growth of beard. His eyes were the rheumy green-brown of dung from a dog on a bad diet. Sweat coated his face, giving it a shiny glow. From the way he grunted and wheezed, and the stiff way he crouched against the cabin, sweating profusely, his jaw held taut and his eyes narrowed, Stillman could tell he was in a great deal of pain.

Stillman's eyes dropped to the man's right leg, the back and side of which were coated with dried blood. This was the man he'd shot in the ass. He must have dragged himself back here when the others had gone after Stillman.

"How ya doin', Rafe?" Stillman said. "Been looking for you."

"You found me, you son of a fuckin' bitch. And now you're gonna die—nice and slow."

"Hold it, Rafe," Claude said, holding up his hand. "I get first crack at him."

Intervening like a benevolent schoolmaster, Billingsley said, "Boys, boys, you'll *each* get a crack at him." He grinned at Stillman, lifting onto the balls of his feet in pure, unabashed delight. He turned to Claude.

"Take him into the corral. I want you to fight him, one at a time. Claude, you can go first. Rafe, you can finish him—any way you want." He turned to the others, a big smile on his face. "No knives, no guns. Just fists. I'll referee." Billingsley lifted the Henry to his waist and thumbed back the hammer.

"He shot me in the ass, goddamnit!" Rafe yelled. "I need a doctor."

"You've lasted this long, Rafe, you'll last a few more hours," Billingsley told the wounded man indulgently. The other men were filing toward the corral, talking among themselves and laughing with anticipation, giddy at how the tables had so suddenly turned in their favor.

Billingsley poked the Henry into Stillman's side. "Move."

The lawman headed for the corral, feeling suddenly pinned between a rock and a hard place. He could see no way out of his present fix. He wished he'd told Leon to look for him at a certain time. He knew the deputy would search for him sooner or later, but since Stillman hadn't specified a time for his return, it could very well be later.

Too much later.

Even in the improbable event he was able to whip all five men Billingsley was about to throw at him, Rafe Paul would still finish him—with the pistol the wounded gunman clung to as though his life depended on it.

The Henry poked Stillman harshly in the back, nudging him into the corral. One of Billingsley's men was letting the horses into another section by a back gate. The horses whinnied and clomped around until the man had them hazed through the open gate, swinging his hat at them and coaxing them with brusque commands. Manes ruffling, the horses trotted into the rear section, a dust cloud lifting in their wake, streaked with the burnished copper of the falling sun.

Then the man closed the gate, latched it with a barbed wire loop, and came across the corral to join his brethren standing with their backs to the rails, rolling cigarettes and regarding Stillman with dark smiles.

Stillman faced them sourly, feeling like a Christian just led up from the cobbled bowels of the Coliseum. Grunting and wheezing, Rafe Paul ducked through the corral. Hand on his hip and looking whiter than ever, he stumbled to the water trough, turned around, and fell into it backward, sending water splashing over the sides. It didn't take long for the water in the trough to turn a light cherry red.

"Okay, Claude—he's all yours," Billingsley barked.

Billingsley sat atop the corral, shiny black boots with square toes hooked over the rail beneath him. Stillman's Henry rifle lay across his knees. He lit a long nine, grinning as he puffed smoke and blew out the match.

Claude tossed away the quirly he'd been smoking, gave his hat to the man beside him, shrugged out of his vest, and moved toward Stillman eagerly. Stillman let his rage boil to the surface as he watched the carnivorous grin stretch across the big, sloppy man's thick-lipped mouth. Something in Stillman's face stopped the man dead in his tracks.

"Okay," he said, suddenly wary. He pointed at his nose. "You stay away from my face, you hear? You even touch my nose, I'm gonna kill you."

The other men laughed. Stillman smiled, crouching and bringing up his fists.

"Come and get it, Claude."

The man crouched, snarling and raising his balled fists. He and Stillman circled once, sidestepping, feinting. Then Claude lunged forward with a right jab, and Stillman hit him on the nose.

The man backed up as though he'd been hit in the chest with a sledgehammer, bending over and grabbing his face with both hands.

"Oh, *goddamn!*" he cried, voice muffled by his hands. "I'm gonna kill you, you son of a bitch!"

"That had to smart."

Shouting, the man dropped his hands from his face and bulled toward Stillman. Stillman saw that the bandage on his nose was red. He stepped aside, grabbed Claude by the scruff of his neck, and flung him face first to the ground.

Claude turned and came up, still raging. Just as he got to his feet, fists balled, Stillman took two quick steps toward him, swung his right fist into his gut, doubling him over, then brought his left knee up into his face.

He felt something give way there. Looking down, he saw his jeans over his knee were dark red. Claude was on the ground, rolling, his hands on his face. He wasn't raging anymore. The only sounds he made were the sounds of an exhausted man trying to catch his breath.

Then a high-pitched wheeze rattled up from his chest. There was a sucking sound. When he took his hands

away from his nose for a moment, Stillman saw that his
nose had been flattened against his face once again—
but in the opposite direction from last time.

Claude turned onto his hands and knees and aired his
paunch on the dried horse dung and hard-packed dirt of
the corral floor.

"Okay, you're done, Claude," Billingsley called from
his perch atop the corral. "What's more, you're fired,
you can't put on a better show than that. Clear your
things out of the bunkhouse and get the hell out of here.
Next!"

The remaining four riders looked at one another, hesitating. Then the smallest got thrust out of the group,
toward Stillman, who was crouched in a fighting position in the middle of the corral, fists raised. He was fired
up now, feeling the angry burn broil up from his loins.
He thought he could lick every last one of them.

He didn't know what he'd do after that, when Billingsley and Rafe Paul would be facing him armed, but
he didn't care. He was too busy concentrating on the
wiry man, about twenty-two or twenty-three, with long-
ish blond curls brushing his shoulders. The kid whipped
off his hat and strode to Stillman with an air of sudden
resolve, swallowing his fear.

He gave Stillman a harder time than the lawman had
expected. He was young, but obviously experienced, and
while light, he was muscular. His fists packed a wallop,
and he was fast on his feet. Stillman felt himself tiring,
following the kid around the corral and jabbing at air
most of the time.

The fight lasted a good fifteen minutes, though it felt
longer. Stillman dropped to a knee once, with a cut

above his eye and an angry welt on his cheek. Then he finally landed a solid blow to the kid's face and followed it up with a jab that rolled his eyes back in his head and sent him staggering back into the fence.

The kid hung there for a minute, half-consciously trying to stay upright, and groaning with the effort. Finally he went lights-out and hit the ground on his ass.

Stillman bent over with his hands on his thighs, trying to catch his breath.

Billingsley yelled, "Next!"

Leon halted his horse at a bend in the trail leading to the Billingsley ranch, and squinted his eyes at the wooded slope on his right.

A big, unfinished house sat on the ridge top, its unpainted lumber burnished copper by the quickly descending sun, its glassless windows black as caves. It wasn't the house which currently piqued the deputy's interest, however. His eyes were focused on something in the woods below it.

Frowning, he reached into his saddlebags, produced his field glasses, and brought them to his eyes.

"What is it?" Fay asked him, drawing her horse alongside his.

Leon lowered the glasses and pointed. "Is that Sweets?"

"Let me see," Fay said. She stared through the glasses for several seconds, then turned to Leon sharply. "Sure enough, let's go!"

She handed the glasses back to Leon and reined her horse toward the woods. Leon reached out for the black's bridle and held it tight, jerking the animal's head back. "Wait now, wait now, Mrs. Stillman," he urged, keeping his voice low. "You can't just go storming over there."

"Leon, Ben is here," Fay said impatiently. "That's his horse. Jody must have given it to him."

"And that up there is Billingsley's house," Leon returned in a raspy whisper, nodding at the big, peaked structure on the ridge. "Now we'd be copper-riveted fools to go stormin' into that bailiwick without thinkin' it through."

"Leon, Ben could be over there *injured*," Fay beseeched him, her eyes wide with fear and worry. With a harsh tug on the reins, she broke loose from Leon's grasp, and spurred the black off the trail and into the grassy dip below the woods, toward the woods themselves.

"Shit," Leon groused, spurring after her.

He'd known that allowing her to ride with him out to the Billingsley place had been a mistake, but there'd been nothing he could do about it. She'd been dead set on coming, either with him or alone. He just hoped he could find Ben *and* keep his wife from getting shot.

"Mrs. Stillman—Fay—*please*," Leon called to her mournfully, trying to keep his voice low. She was off her horse and scouring the woods around the bay, who eyed the newcomers with guarded, sidelong glances.

Leon dismounted and quickly tethered his horse to a tree, then turned and started after Fay, intending to hogtie her if he had to. He stopped as she approached him.

"I don't see him. He must be up there," she said, nodding at the ridgetop through the muddy wash of woods climbing the hill.

She turned to climb the slope. Leon grabbed her arm and turned her back around. "Listen," he ordered, angry now. He was not going to let the fool woman get herself shot—no matter how stubbornly her will seemed to be pulling her in that direction. "I'm in charge here, and I told you back in town the only way I'd let you come out here was if you followed my orders. Now if you don't do as I say—no disrespect intended—I'm gonna tie you to that tree over there!" He thrust his arm at an aspen.

The obstinate determination in Fay's eyes withdrew behind a film of capitulation. Her face crumpled. "I'm just so worried," she cried, gazing deep into the deputy's eyes.

"I am, too," Leon told her commandingly. "And I aim to find Ben and give him a hand. But we have to slow down and think things through, and you have to follow my lead. 'Cause if you don't—"

"I know, I know," Fay nodded. "You'll tie me to the tree. I understand." She stood with her eyes demurely lowered, yielding to Leon's authority.

McMannigle shucked his Spencer seven-shot repeater from his saddle boot. "Now we're gonna climb this hill—slow, keeping our eyes peeled. At the top, you're going to wait in the woods while I check out the house. You're gonna stay put until I say the coast is clear. Understand?"

"I understand, Leon. Please hurry."

A horse whinnied behind them. Quickly jacking a shell in his Winchester's breech, Leon turned to see a red-haired man in a derby hat approach on a skewbald horse. It was Doc Evans, holding a two-barrel shotgun, butt snugged against his thigh. The trotting horse was sweat-matted and blowing.

Leon off-cocked the Winchester and dropped it to his side.

"Wait here," he told Fay through a sigh. He walked over to meet the doctor, a question in his eyes.

Climbing heavily out of the saddle, Evans said with customary self-deprecation, "I figured if she was going to tag along, it was the least I could do." He looked at Fay. "Hard to sit back in my easy chair knowing a woman's out here doing a man's work."

"You any good with that thing?" Leon said, regarding the two-bore skeptically.

"As a young lad, I used to bag quite a few pheasants and ducks with it. That good enough?"

"I guess it has to be," McMannigle said fatefully, more than a little leery of his sudden "posse." He thought he'd be more effective alone, but Fay and the good doctor were here and there was nothing he could do about that now.

"This way, and stay behind me," he told the doctor, turning and shaking his head as he climbed the hill. He felt like a mother duck with an unruly brood on her heels.

Near the ridgetop, Leon lifted his hand to the others, halting them, then got down and crawled on his hands and knees to the brow of the hill. Removing his round-brimmed black hat, he shuttled a cautious gaze over the ridge. The house towered there, its turrets and peaks standing dark against the fading sky. A swallow flew out a window and angled into the woods, chirping.

The bird's presence told Leon the house was abandoned, but he couldn't ignore it until he knew for sure. He turned to Fay and the doctor, crouched behind him, regarding him expectantly. "Wait here."

He ran to the house with his Winchester clutched before him, listened through the raw wood walls, then stepped through the door. Inside, all was quiet, but he could hear voices outside, on the opposite side of the house from Fay and the doctor. Leon moved to an outside door, stood against the wall, and peered through the opening.

In a corral about a hundred yards down the sloping grade from the house, two men were fighting. It was hard to tell from this distance, but one looked like Stillman. With his bent knees and slumped shoulders, he looked as though he'd been through hell, and wasn't far from finished.

Leon surveyed the area, counting five other men watching the fight. Those weren't the best odds, but Leon thought he could beat them if he kept the element of surprise on his side of the table.

He went back to Fay and the doctor. "They're on the other side of the house, about a hundred yards away," he said. "Follow me and keep your heads down." He wanted to keep Fay here, out of harm's way, but he knew there was no way she'd stay.

In single file, Leon out front and Fay in the middle, the three made their way across the hill, until the bunkhouse and the barn were between them and the corral. Then they descended the hill to the barn, and stepped inside.

Leon turned to Fay. "Mrs. Stillman, you wait here." His dark eyes were wide, brimming with gravity. He would not take no for an answer. Getting the message, Fay nodded.

To the doctor, Leon said, "Let's go," and started toward the other end of the barn.

The voices had grown louder. Leon could hear them clearly now. One man was chuckling. There was the thump and smack of knuckles against flesh, and the grunts of air expunged from weakening lungs. Angry curses lifted on the evening-quiet air.

At the doors, Leon gestured for the doctor to move off to his right, shotgun ready. They would come up behind the party in the corral, quietly, and take them all by surprise.

To that end, Leon brought the Winchester to his shoulder, eased back the hammer, and moved toward the corral, his gaze planted inside, where one man was holding Stillman by both arms. Another man was punching him in the face and stomach.

Stillman's face was bloody and his hair was disheveled, the sweat-soaked, salt-and-pepper mass covering his forehead and eyes. His eyes were half-open, as though he were barely conscious.

The older gent on the corral fence, with Stillman's rifle across his knees, said, "How do you feel now, Sheriff? Wishin' you would have left well enough alone. I told you no one messes with Norman Billingsley—not with the kind of money I brought up from Texas." Thoughtfully, he puffed on his long-nine. "Hell, I think I'm gonna change 'Clantick' to 'Billingsley.' What do you think, boys?"

Leon said, "Well, if you're askin' me, I think Billingsley sounds a little fruity."

Billingsley and the other men turned to him sharply, Billingsley lifting the Henry from his knees.

"Uh-uh, Norman," warned Doc Evans, behind him.

Leon looked at the men in the corral. The two working on Stillman had froze. They watched Leon with mute rage in their eyes, sweat streaking the grime on their faces.

"Who in the hell are you?" the one who'd been punching Ben yelled.

"Name's McMannigle," Leon said. "I'm the new deputy here. Anyone armed?"

The man holding Stillman suddenly let him go. Ben fell and rolled sideways with a groan. Leon's eyes darted to the man in the water trough. The man wasn't looking at him.

"You in the water trough—turn around."

"He's injured," Billingsley said. "Stillman shot him in the ass."

"Turn around, anyway."

Leon couldn't see clearly from this angle, but the man's right shoulder moved. Then, just as it dawned on him that the man was extending a gun toward Stillman, a small-caliber pistol cracked. The head of the man in the water trough jerked to the side, so that his right ear slapped his right shoulder. The head bounced back up, and Leon saw blood dampen the hair on the side of his head.

The man lifted his chin, said, "Aaa—aah," in a gurgling voice, and lay back in the trough, arms falling over the sides. His right hand opened, and the pistol fell to the ground.

Leon turned to his left, where Fay stood at the end of

the corral, peering through the rails, pistol extended. She wore a serious, half-shocked expression on her face. As if suddenly roused from a dream, she holstered the pistol, bent through the corral, and ran to Ben.

"You men, come on out here," Leon ordered the two uglies in the corral. There were two other men, passed out on the ground, but they were incapacitated. Leon looked at the older gent perched atop the corral, whom the doctor had already relieved of Stillman's Henry.

"Get down."

"What the hell you think *you're* gonna do?" Billingsley barked.

Leon shrugged theatrically. "Oh, I don't know . . . maybe . . . throw your fat white ass in jail?"

He glanced at the doctor, still puffing his stogey.

The doctor grinned.

21

One month later . . .

Stillman and McMannigle stood before the jailhouse, side-by-side, as two federal deputy marshals led Bernard McFadden and Norman Billingsley toward the train station. Both men's hands and feet were shackled. Each man was cuffed to the wrist of one of the marshals.

"Now, ain't that a pretty sight?" Leon asked Stillman.

"That has to be one of the prettier sights I've seen on the Hi-Line—in recent days, anyway," Stillman agreed.

Billingsley turned around awkwardly, nearly tripping on his chains, and made an obscene gesture at Stillman and McMannigle. Then one of the marshals jerked him back around, and he continued on his forced march to the depot, where a train was waiting to take him and his associate to the territorial pen at Deer Lodge.

They'd both been sentenced to ten years hard labor for murder, assault, and about five other things for which Stillman and the district attorney had written them up. The trial had taken two weeks. A jury of twelve from Clantick, in the count of a visiting judge, had taken three days to convict both men of most of the counts, including murder.

"It was touch-and-go there for a while," Stillman said, shaking his head. His bruises had healed, for the most part, but he still had a nasty scab on his left cheekbone, and a fair-sized bruise on his right temple.

"Yeah, well, a lot of people in this town—and a few members of the jury—hated to see them go," Leon said. "For good or bad, they helped this town prosper."

"I wonder what's going to happen now," Stillman said, watching the two prisoners disappear in the crowd down the street. Billingsley's surviving riders, tried separately from their employer and the banker, had been transported two days ago.

"Well, for one thing, you two are taking a lady to dinner." Both men turned to see Fay standing there in a long pink gown, with a pink parasol above her lovely head, black curls brushing her shoulders and cleavage laid bare by the dress's low neckline.

Stillman turned to Leon. "Did we say that?"

"I don't remember saying that," Leon said, playing along. "Besides, this woman looks a little too good to sit at the same table with this badge-totin' darky."

"Or this badge-totin' whitey," Stillman added.

Fay stepped between them and turned around, grabbing their arms and leading them off toward the Boston. "Come along, boys," she said. "With McFadden and Billingsley off to the hoosegow, we've got some celebrating to do."

"I don't know," Leon said, as Fay ushered him and Stillman along. "We might have arrested ourselves out of a job. With those two gone, this town might not need us anymore."

"Don't talk too loud," Stillman said, as pleased as Leon by how things had turned out. "One of the city councilmen might overhear—" Stillman stopped, something across the street catching his eye.

"What is it?" Fay said, gazing up at him curiously.

"Humperdink."

"Who?"

Stillman gestured at the bearded, well-dressed man supervising two odd-jobbers wrestling a steamer trunk into the back of a two-seater buggy across the street, before the building in which Humperdink's office had been housed.

"Packin' up and shovin' off," Leon said.

"Where's he going?" Fay asked.

Stillman tipped his hat brim back. "I heard he was heading south to Winifred, where he has family. No point in hanging around here—since he's been disbarred and all. Being in cahoots with McFadden and Billingsley didn't do much for his career."

Stillman's eyes were still on the former judge. When the two men had finished loading the trunks into the buggy, Humperdink handed each a coin, then climbed onto the buggy, awkwardly maneuvering his lanky frame beneath the canopy decorated with black tassels.

He caught sight of the three regarding him from across the street, and stiffened. His face lost its color, and he turned away, sitting on the padded leather seat and taking up his reins. He clucked to the two matched blacks in the traces, and quickly put them in a spanking trot, moving west down First.

"Why do I feel sorry for that son of a bitch?" Stillman asked no one in particular.

"Because you're human," Fay said, setting off down the boardwalk again, Stillman and Leon in tow.

Their table in the Boston's dining room had been re-served. Jody and Crystal were already there, dressed for the occasion. Seeing the three newcomers, Jody stood and smiled, looking dapper with his pomaded hair and wearing a string tie and jacket.

As Ben, Fay, and Leon made their way to the table, two businessmen in broadcloth suits glared at them, scoffed, threw back their drinks, stood, and headed scowling for the door.

"Friends of yours?" Crystal asked Stillman.

"You don't have to guess whose side they were on," Leon remarked.

Stillman nodded as he held Fay's chair. "McFadden and Billingsley had considerable interest in their busi-nesses. The conviction ruined them."

"They did look less than pleased," Fay allowed, ac-cepting the menu offered by the maître d', a willowy, effete-looking gent in a white apron, paisley waistcoat, and with a black spit curl plastered across his forehead.

When he'd handed out menus and recited the eve-ning's specials, he produced matches from a pocket in his apron and lit the tall, white candle centered in a bouquet of fresh bluebonnets. "And just so you know, gentlemen and ladies," the man said, nodding at Fay and Crystal, "your meals will be on the house tonight. It's the hotel's way of saying thanks for ridding Clantick of the likes of"—he made a gesture with his hands, obvi-ously indicating Billingsley and McFadden—"of *those*." He shook the curl from his eye and headed for the kitchen.

"Someone likes us," Leon said.

"Don't worry, most of the town's on your side," Jody

assured him and Ben. "I've been asking around. It's just going to take some folks a little getting used to operating on the up-and-up."

"They better get used to it," Stillman said through a sigh. " 'Cause we're here to stay. Aren't we, Fay?"

Fay frowned and stared thoughtfully at the shimmering candle flame emitting a thin stream of black smoke. "A month ago, I wasn't so sure."

A dark look entered her eyes. Fighting it off, she reached across the table, squeezed Ben's hand, and smiled at Jody. "But I've decided I like it here."

"I believe I've eaten a meal like that only once before," Leon said with a sated sigh. "I was seein' a foxy white woman at the time, and her husband had money. This girl was so—"

He glanced around at the group—Stillman, Fay, Jody, and Crystal—regarding him expectantly. It was dark on the boardwalk, and the oil lamps had been lit on either side of the hotel's double doors. Piano music lifted from one of the saloons down the street.

"Oh, well . . . never mind," Leon said, chagrined. "Guess it ain't exac'ly the kind of story I should tell with ladies present."

The women smiled. Stillman laughed. Jody stepped forward and shook Ben's and Leon's hands. "We best be heading back to the ranch," he said. "Tomorrow's another day. Thanks for inviting us to the celebration," he said to Stillman.

"There'd've been no celebration without you two," Stillman said to him and Crystal, who stepped forward and gave him a parting hug. "And thanks again for Sweets. That was quite a surprise."

"Pa would've wanted you to have him," Jody said, moving to the buckboard wagon tied at the hitch rack.

Crystal hugged Fay and Leon, then climbed onto the buckboard behind her husband. "I'll ride out there in a day or two and see what you've done to the new place, maybe do some fishing," Stillman called as Jody slapped the reins against the two mismatched horses pulling the wagon.

"We'll watch for you," Jody said.

When the wagon had drifted out of sight, Fay grabbed Ben's arm. "Escort a lady home?"

Stillman looked at Leon, then shuttled his gaze to Fay. "I've got a little paperwork I have to finish up before I can call it a night," he said regretfully.

Fay sighed and let go his arm. "I figured as much."

"I'll see you in a couple hours."

"I'll wait up with a book," Fay said, and kissed her husband's cheek. "Good night, Leon." She opened the door and slipped into the hotel.

Stillman turned to Leon, who shrugged and sighed.

Wordlessly, they walked down the porch steps to the boardwalk, and strolled over to the jailhouse, sitting dark and alone under a sky full of stars. Stillman unlocked the door, went inside, and lit the lamp on his desk, looking around with a hand on his pistol grip. He turned to Leon standing in the open doorway. His hand, too, was on the grip of his holstered gun.

Stillman shrugged and said, "Well, I reckon I'll try to finish up some paperwork."

Leon cleared his throat. "Yeah, well . . . I'll head on

over to the Goliad, make sure everyone's abidin' by our no-gun policy. I'll see ya later."

"See ya," Stillman said, watching McMannigle turn, walk outside, and close the door behind him.

Stillman yawned, loosened his string tie, removed his corduroy jacket—it was a hot, muggy July night—and sat down behind his desk, opening the small, wood box in which his pen and ink were stored.

Outside, across the street, three people stood in the dark alley between a harness shop and a dentist's office, peering at the jailhouse's lighted window, behind which the vague form of Stillman could be seen, slumped over his desk.

"Okay," Bob Andrews said through a long sigh. "We got him just where we want him. Everyone know what to do?"

E. L. "Scratch" Lawson and Evelyn nodded.

"Remember, Evelyn," Bob said. "Someone stole your purse a few days ago. You kept thinking you just lost it, and you thought it'd show up, but it hasn't, and now you think some grubliner stole it."

"I know, Bob," Evelyn said distantly, staring at the jail.

"Let me see how ya look." Bob turned her toward him brusquely and regarded her bosom, opulently revealed by her low-cut gown. As she stood there stoically regarding the jail, he grabbed her breasts, adjusting them, and pulled the fabric down to just above her nipples.

He smiled. "There, that should keep him distracted. He might be married to the prettiest little thing this side of the Mississippi, but he'll still be givin' those a gander—long enough for Scratch and me to bust in and drill him, anyways."

Scratch eyed Evelyn's breasts and snickered, forgetting for a moment the fearful task he had before him. Bob cuffed his ear. "Get your mind on your job!" he snarled. "You ready?"

Scratch nodded, rubbing his ear.

"Go then," Bob said.

Scratch moved off down the alley and disappeared around the corner. When he'd waited ten minutes, long enough for Scratch to have gotten into position, Bob gave Evelyn a harsh pat across her plump buttocks.

"Okay, do your thing, girl."

Evelyn inhaled deeply, cleared her throat, and moved out of the alley and into the street, toward the jail. Bob watched her move past the hitch rack and knock on the door. A second later she opened the door and went in. Through the window, Bob could see Stillman rise. He and Evelyn stood there for several minutes. Then Evelyn sat in a chair before his desk. Stillman returned to the one behind it.

Bob's grin belied his anxiety.

He unholstered his .45, gave the cylinder a spin, re-holstered the weapon, and headed across the street to the jail, giving the window a wide berth. He went to the building's west corner, and peered down the length of the jailhouse to the rear. He couldn't see Scratch back there—it was too dark—but he figured there was enough light on First for Scratch to see him.

He lifted his arm, waving, and whistled once, softly. He counted to sixty, giving Scratch enough time to enter the jailhouse through the back door and make his way to the front office.

He unholstered his gun, stepped quietly toward the door, and flung it open. Stillman was sitting behind the desk, Evelyn across from him. Scratch was peering around the door leading to the cells.

"Now!" Bob shouted, and he and Scratch opened up on Stillman, each man sending one round after another through the sheriff's chest and back, knocking the man forward onto his desk, then back in his chair, and sideways against the wall.

Suddenly, Bob stopped firing. His angry snarl was replaced by a frown. The blood left his face, and he suddenly felt hot as a fully stoked stove.

"Is he dead?" Scratch asked, but Bob didn't hear him. He was too busy staring numbly, through the thick powder smoke, at the bloodless, boneless, faceless figure— no more than a straw dummy in jeans and a gingham shirt!—slumped against the wall. Bits of straw shone through the holes in the clothes.

Bob turned to Evelyn, sitting there stiffly, facing the desk. Only she was no more Evelyn than Stillman was Stillman. It was a straw dummy dressed like the other.

"Why . . ." Scratch muttered, moving into the room, a horrified expression crumpling his dark, unshaven features. "Why . . . that ain't Stillman. . . ."

Bob saw someone move through the door behind Scratch. It was Stillman, a Henry rifle raised to his shoulder. Bob froze, felt his knees melt and his heart pound. "Drop the gun, Bob," Stillman said.

Scratch jerked, lifting his pistol. Someone behind Bob said, "You, too, Scratch." Bob turned a glance over his shoulder. The deputy was standing there with his pistol aimed at Scratch. The black man's eyes slid to Bob for just a second, warningly, then returned to Scratch, who returned the deputy's look, his face expressing a mix of sadness, horror, and disbelief.

At length, Scratch's eyes slid to Bob. "I don't wanna die, Bob," he cried. Watching Bob, he bent slowly forward and set his pistol on the floor, then slumped to his knees and laced his hands behind his head.

"What about you, Bob?" Stillman said. "Do you want to die?"

Bob hated himself for his unspoken answer. He was a coward. Knowing what his father would say if he saw him now—"You yellow-bellied little pecker!"—he gave a sigh, expressing all the sadness of his wretched being—and set the pistol on the floor between his feet.

"That was the right decision, Bob," Stillman told him.

Someone else entered the room behind the lawman. Bob's face remained expressionless as Evelyn stepped out from behind Stillman to face him, her cold, hard eyes locking on his.

Bob shook his head, slowly, uncomprehendingly. "You . . . told . . . Why . . . ?"

Evelyn just stared at him, her eyes the living picture of loathing.

"You never should have gotten rough with her, Bob," Leon said. "To get back at you, she came to us and spilled your whole plan in our laps."

Evelyn inhaled deeply, her eyes still on Bob. "You didn't even need to do it, Bob. Your old man is dead. The sheriff shot him." A faint smile creased her lips.

Bob's face turned mean. "You whore," he snarled.

Evelyn lifted her hand and swung it hard across his face. His left eye watered from the pain.

Bob ground his teeth together and lunged toward her. "Why, you—"

Stillman intervened, grabbing Bob by the shoulder and shoving him toward the cell block. "You're finished with that stuff, Bob. You're going to have a good long time to reconsider your treatment of the lady."

With his drawn revolver, Leon ushered Scratch down the cell block behind Bob. When both men were locked up, Leon and Stillman returned to the office, where Evelyn sat in the chair before the desk. Her stand-in was on the floor behind her.

Stillman returned the cell keys to the peg beside the door, walked across the room, and hiked a hip on his desk, regarding Evelyn sadly. Leon stood by the stove.

"You did the right thing," Stillman told her. "As a matter of fact, I'm much obliged."

"What am I going to do now?" the girl said weakly. Tears rolled down her cheeks. "I don't have anyone . . . no place to go . . . no money. . . ."

"I talked to Sam Wah, the Chinese gent who owns the restaurant down the street," Stillman said. "He said he had enough business these days to warrant hiring a waitress."

The girl lifted her head to regard Stillman expectantly. "You . . . talked to him . . . about *me*?"

"Sure, I did. You're a fine girl. All you need is a break. Now, I doubt Sam Wah can pay you much, and I know waitressing isn't the best job in the—"

"I'll take it," Evelyn said, eagerly.

Stillman turned to Leon and smiled, then turned his

smile to the girl. "I figured you would. It's a start, any-way."

"It's better than going back to Helena," Evelyn said. "Oh, it's . . . it's much better than that!"

She stared at Stillman for several seconds. Then she bounded to her feet, ran to him, and threw her arms around his neck, hugging him. Stillman smiled and patted her back. When the girl pulled away, she dropped her eyes, embarrassed.

"I'm . . . I'm just so grateful," she said, her voice breaking and her shoulders jerking as she broke down in tears.

Stillman went to his desk and opened a drawer. "Here's a little money—it's just a loan, you understand; I expect to have it back once Sam starts paying you. It's not much but it's enough to get you a cheap room and a few square meals."

Evelyn accepted the money graciously. "Thank you, Sheriff," she said, wiping her cheeks with her hands. "I don't know how to thank you."

"You can thank me by being at Wah's at seven o'clock tomorrow. He opens early." Stillman winked at her. "And by the way, I like my eggs sunny-side-up."

When the girl had left, after thanking Stillman a half dozen more times, Leon picked up the bullet-riddled straw dummies and stood with each under an arm. "I reckon I best get these scarecrows back to Mrs. Bjorn-son, or she'll be sendin' us a bill for the corn the crows eat out of her garden."

He chuckled, headed for the door, and stopped, swing-ing his head to Stillman. "You know what, Ben? You're sentimental."

"No, just practical," Stillman said, eyeing the door through which Evelyn had left the jailhouse. "Giving that kid a break now means less trouble for me later."

"You can explain it all you want, but I still say you're sentimental."

Stillman turned to Leon with an expression of mock anger. "Don't you have work to do, Deputy?"

Leon grinned and shrugged. "I think we've done cleaned up the town!"

The sound of breaking glass lifted from outside. Stillman and McMannigle ran out the door and gazed up the street, the straw-bleeding scarecrows still under Leon's arms. Before a brightly lit saloon, a crowd was forming around two fighting cowboys.

Stillman sighed. "No, we just got rid of the big shots," he said. "The real work's still ahead."

Leon dropped the scarecrows with a sigh and followed Stillman up the street.

EPILOGUE

The next morning, Crystal awoke later than usual. Sunlight flooded the bedroom. Yawning, she turned to see if Jody had slept in, too. He hadn't. His side of the bed was empty, the single sheet thrown back.

Feeling more tired than usual—feeling downright fatigued, in fact—Crystal pushed herself to a sitting position and sat there for several minutes, holding her blond hair back from her forehead and yawning, trying to come awake.

She stood, looked around groggily for her clothes, and dressed. Brushing her hair as she left the bedroom and headed for the kitchen, she glanced out the living room window and stopped. Beyond the window, Jody was standing by his father's grave, under the cottonwood about seventy yards east of the barn. The morning light flashed like pennies on the churning leaves of the tree towering above him. Jody's horse stood nearby, its reins in Jody's hand. Jody was looking down at the humped grave and stone marker.

Crystal stood in the window, watching her husband thoughtfully. Finally she moved to the cabin door, opened it, and went out. She crossed the barnyard and strode across the pasture, through the dew-beaded timothy Jody had already cut once this season.

Jody looked up and saw her coming. She waved. He

waved back and stood there, watching her come, the morning breeze blowing her hair. "Good morning," she said, approaching the grave.

"Mornin'."

"Sorry I slept in. Did you get breakfast?"

"I made a bacon sandwich. You all right?"

Crystal stood next to him, rubbing her shoulder against him, soaking up his heat. It was a cool morning for July. "Sure. Why?"

"I heard you get up twice last night and use the privy."

Crystal shrugged. "I reckon I drank too much wine. You know I can't drink that late and sleep right." She glanced at her husband and smiled tenderly. "You have a good talk with your pa?"

"Yeah, I reckon. I sure wish he could talk back, though."

Crystal's smile faded. A troubled look entered her eyes. "Jody . . ." She wasn't sure how to continue.

He frowned, sweeping back a wing of hair from her face with the back of his hand. "What is it, honey?"

"I . . . rode over to my pa's grave a while back. I put flowers on it. I think I'd like to start tending the grave some—at least once a year. On his birthday." She looked at him, feeling guilty and abashed. Her eyes were concerned, afraid of what Jody would say about this.

He chuffed and smiled, looking relieved. "That's what you wanted to tell me?"

"Jody, he killed your father. It's hard for me to know how to feel about him. Part of me hates him more than I ever hated anyone, and then on the other hand, I feel like . . . this closeness . . . to him." Her eyes swept the horizon and drifted back to Jody. "I feel guilty about it."

"Crystal Johnson, do you really think I wouldn't want you tending your father's grave?" Jody looked angry.

"He killed your father, Jody. . . :"

"He's dead, for godsakes, Crystal. He paid for what he did." He took Crystal in his arms and pressed her head to his chest. "And I want you to stop paying for what he did. It had nothing to do with you. He was your father and he's dead and you can stop paying for his sins. I've forgiven him."

Crystal's shoulders shook, and she sobbed against his chest. Jody squeezed her shoulders. "Next year, we'll both ride over there, and put up a stone."

"You don't have to do that for him."

"I'm not doing it for him. I'm doing it for you."

Crystal smiled and pushed away from Jody, but kept both her hands on his chest. Her face was red and tear-washed. "I've got something else to tell you, but I wanted to tell you that first."

"Uh-oh," Jody kidded. "You pick out another horse to buy?"

Crystal smiled. "I think you're going to be a father."

Jody stared at her, his eyes widening.

"I think that's what's been making me so tired lately, and why I've been getting up so many times to use the privy."

Jody gazed at her and took both her arms in his hands. "Really? You really think so?"

Crystal shrugged and nodded. "I don't know what else it could be. I talked to Mrs.—"

Jody cut loose with a whoop, spooking his horse, which slipped its reins from Jody's hands and jumped several feet away before lowering its head again to crop grass. He lifted Crystal off her feet, laughing and whooping, then set her back down and kissed her.

Crystal smiled and laughed, tears returning to her eyes.

"You know what I think we should do?" Jody said. "I think we should take the day off and go have us a picnic. Let's pack a lunch and head up to Long John Butte, and spread us a blanket in that meadow. You know the one I mean—"

"Jody," Crystal said, folding her arms and giving her husband an admonishing look.

"What?" Jody said, incredulous.

"We're going to have a whole passel of kids. If we stop work to celebrate another bun in my oven, we'll never get anything done!"

"But, Crystal, this is special—"

"You get to work, Jody Harmon. You're going to have a whole cabin full of wailing brats to feed. Then you'll see how special it is."

Jody opened his mouth to speak. Crystal raised a schoolmarmish eyebrow, cowing him. His shoulders slumped. "All right, Crystal," he said. "Whatever you say."

Crystal brightened. "Now, that's what I like to hear."

"You're a hard woman, Mrs. Harmon."

"Only because I have to be, Mr. Harmon."

He turned to his horse, stopped, and turned back to regard Crystal expectantly. "You're sure?"

"I'm sure," she replied with a smile.

"*Goddamn,*" Jody said, giving her a quick, parting kiss on the lips. "I'm gonna be a poppa." He turned to his horse, grabbed the reins, and climbed into the saddle. "I'll see you at five," he told Crystal.

"Make it four," Crystal said, containing a grin.

Jody looked at her frowning.

"Do you want to go to Long John Butte or don't you?" she asked. "We used to fool around there, remember?"

Smiling coquettishly, she turned and headed back toward the cabin. Jody watched her for several seconds, grinning, happier than he'd ever been in his life. Then he reined his buckskin across the creek and up the opposite bank, laughing.

About the Author

Peter Brandvold was born and raised in North Dakota and educated at the Univerisity of North Dakota and the University of Arizona. He taught for five years on the Rocky Boy Indian Reservation in northern Montana and now lives with his wife on their turn-of-the-century farmstead near Underwood, Minnesota.